MURDER IN THE EMBASSY

Tom BWall

1933.

MURDER IN THE EMBASSY

MURDER
IN THE EMBASSY

By
DIPLOMAT

GEORGE G. HARRAP & CO. LTD.
LONDON   **BOMBAY**   **SYDNEY**

First published in this Series in 1933
by GEORGE G. HARRAP & CO. LTD.
39–41 Parker Street, Kingsway, London, W.C.2

Made and Printed in Great Britain by Purnell & Sons
Paulton (Somerset) and London

I

THE CORPSE IN THE LIBRARY

PRINCE HOJO, cousin of the Emperor of Japan, rang for his valet again, impatient at the slight delay which followed his first summons. " Beastly nuisance ! " he exclaimed as he pushed the bell-button. The door into the corridor swung noiselessly open, admitting a servant who carried a silver tray on which were two long, cool-looking glasses.

The two men who were waiting downstairs in the darkened living-room heard the bell ring, once, twice, in the basement. Then they heard the patter of the servant's feet in the corridor. A few minutes later they heard the valet's footsteps patter away. Deep silence brooded over the Japanese Embassy, the deep silence of a midsummer afternoon in a house which has been closed for the season.

The Japanese Embassy was closed, officially. The Ambassador and his staff were spending the summer in Manchester, officially. The Chancery offices in the basement still acknowledged the daily attendance of one or two clerks and specialists and of the Secretary who had been left to experience the inferno of a

9

Washington summer. But at four o'clock on a Saturday afternoon in August the most docile of clerks, enthusiastic of specialists, and disillusioned of Secretaries are not to be found in a Chancery, when the Ambassador is five hundred odd miles away on the North Shore of Massachusetts. The Embassy was heavily shuttered and the blinds were down on the sides facing Sixteenth Street and the Avenue. The whir and honk of motors rounding the Circle sounded faintly. One or two windows opening on to the walled garden to the rear of the building provided ventilation, and the thick walls and high ceilings cooled the room where the Ambassador, Viscount Kondo, and Mr James B. Acorn, the Assistant Secretary of State, were awaiting the arrival of the Secretary himself. Upstairs in the pleasant little library which lay between the upstairs sitting-room and the little anteroom on the Sixteenth Street side Lord Robert Murray, his Britannic Majesty's Chargé d'Affaires ad Interim, was discussing with Prince Hojo the final terms of the agreement which they were about to sign.

It had taken careful and intelligent planning to effect that meeting. Prince Hojo had left Tokio early in June, for a trip across Soviet Russia, a protracted visit in Berlin, and a tour of the Portuguese vineyards.

From Portugal he had gone to the Azores, where it happened that a Japanese merchant vessel bound from Suez to New Orleans had taken aboard a young Japanese student, on the strong representations of the Imperial Consul-General. At New Orleans the young Japanese student had walked ashore past the Customs officials and had boarded a train for the North three hours later. A young Japanese student, hot and soiled from travel, had got off the Pullman at the Union Station in Washington, had very naturally boarded a street-car which bore the label " Mount Pleasant," and descended at Connecticut Avenue and M Street. He had then turned eastward on Rhode Island Avenue, keeping on the shady side until he came to the Embassy. Casually producing a latchkey from his pocket, the young Japanese had walked up the front steps and let himself in. Half an hour later, Prince Hojo, cousin of the Emperor, bathed and wearing fresh whites, had found himself gossiping about Balliol and the Yankees' chance to win the baseball pennant with Bob Murray, *alias* his Britannic Majesty's Chargé d'Affaires ad Interim, and for all necessary purposes a plenipotentiary of considerable power.

No, it had not been simple. Everybody knew that the Ambassador was in Manchester. Everybody knew that Murray himself was spending the summer at York Harbour. Everybody knew that Acorn had taken the midnight train on Friday for New York, and only the porter knew that the Assistant Secretary had got out at Baltimore for a paper and had missed getting on in time. The Secretary of State, of course, was out lecturing in Ohio on " Peace." Nobody knew that he had slipped aboard the Washington Special at Cincinnati after his lecture and had gone back to the Capital. He would speak on Tuesday at Columbus and it was understood that he was visiting friends near Pittsburgh. Not an easy thing to outwit the intelligence systems of a score of public and private agencies and bring together three plenipotentiaries to sign a treaty which would rewrite the map of world-power for a generation.

Acorn cleared his throat and hunched his shoulders aggressively. " I don't know why the Secretary's so late, Mr Ambassador," he grumbled. " The train was on time."

He was very uncomfortable. Perspiration glistened on his red face, his thick fingers drummed on the dust-cloth of his chair. His bull neck felt too tight for his collar. He would have given his life for one of those tall drinks he had seen that Jap valet carrying upstairs a few minutes ago.

The Ambassador said nothing. His parchment face,

with its scraggly black moustache and its impassive
eyes, bespoke a race and tradition to which time and
climate are nothing. He would wait until summoned
by his Imperial Highness or until the Secretary of
State appeared. For that he had his orders.

The door-bell rang, so suddenly and so loudly that
Acorn started. "There he is," he remarked super-
fluously.

There was a patter of feet on the stairs and the valet
appeared. A moment later the Secretary of State was
ushered in, if so mild a word can describe the abrupt
entrance of a little red-faced old gentleman, whose
eyes were snapping and who seemed to be propelled by
a series of discreetly muffled explosions, like an internal-
combustion engine.

"Good afternoon, Mr Ambassador," he snapped.
"Delighted to see you. Family well? That's good.
Everything ready? Hullo, Acorn. Heat's terrible, isn't
it? Taxi had a breakdown and I had to walk the last
three blocks."

The Ambassador remembered that hospitality was
a tradition of the Orient as efficiency was of the West,
and stood balancing in his mind the correct procedure.

"Delighted and honoured by your visit, Mr Secretary," he announced in that curious sing-song which

betrays so many of his race, despite its linguistic achievements. " His Imperial Highness is awaiting you."

" Thanks, Mr Ambassador," the Secretary beamed. " Shall I go upstairs? "

The Ambassador clapped his hands and in a moment the valet appeared. "Kanehira," the diplomat ordered, in English, for the benefit of his guests, " you will announce to his Highness that the Secretary of State is here."

The Secretary pulled a large bandana handkerchief from his pocket and mopped his brow. He took a lightning glance at the bronzes, jades, and woodcuts of priceless authenticity which had made the Embassy the envy and despair of museums. He looked at Acorn searchingly.

"Anybody in the Department know of this? " he demanded.

" Not a soul but yours truly," the Assistant Secretary assured him.

" Ha, that's fine! The Department is the world's best place in which to lose a secret. Bar C.P.I. there's not a soul there that won't tell all to the first reporter who asks them whether it's going to rain to-morrow."

Acorn chuckled. " This time I didn't even tell C.P.I. Ever since Tyler came back from Tokio he's been acting as though he had invented the Japanese Empire for the especial benefit of his bureau. I put something over on him this time."

The Secretary smiled. He knew there was no love lost between the Chief of the Bureau of Current Political Intelligence and the new Assistant Secretary who had been appointed to reorganize the Department. Acorn, before he had been warned that there was such a thing as political intelligence, had issued orders for the abolition of the Bureau—a step which had been followed by such diabolical complications in his work that before a week was out he had re-established the Bureau with full powers and increased funds. The Secretary also knew that this was neither the time nor the place to indulge in office gossip.

Silence fell upon the group, a silence in which even the light footfall of the valet could be heard, as he ascended the stairs to notify Prince Hojo that the Secretary of State had arrived. There was a brief and discreet pause, then a single knock on the door of the upstairs room. Another pause was followed by another knock. There was a renewed patter of footsteps and the valet appeared abruptly. He said something low in Japanese to the Ambassador. The Ambassador started up, then subsided.

"The Prince is still busy, I suppose," he said, apologetically. "He did not answer the knock. In a moment I shall send up again."

"Quite all right with me, Mr Ambassador," the Secretary assured him. "I can wait."

"How is this thing going to affect your Government, anyhow?" he continued. "Last spring I should have said it would have been impossible, the way all your patriots were talking about the Philippines."

The Ambassador smiled suavely. "We have our patriots under perfect control," he said. "They will not trouble us. If a Prince of the Imperial House signs this treaty, they will accept. Some of our extremists, some of the radicals, the Black Dragon Society perhaps, will object, but that will be all. No trouble."

Mr Acorn cleared his throat. It was time, he decided, to show the Ambassador that he too knew what was what in Japanese politics. "The Black Dragons," he said solemnly, "are a sort of Bolshevik organization, aren't they?"

The Ambassador was urbanely positive. "We have no Bolshevists in Japan," he remarked dryly. "The Black Dragons are more like your D.A.R., very patriotic, oh, very, so long as it means that we shall build enough warships to keep the steel industry happy and insult enough foreign nations to make warships necessary. They have no importance where anything big is concerned."

The conversation languished. Feeling that the Prince had been given time enough, the Ambassador clapped his hands again. "Kanehira," he commanded, "inform his Imperial Highness that the Secretary of State is waiting."

The house seemed very still. Traffic on the Avenue had almost ceased. The homeward rush from the Government offices and shops had ended and the return from the country had not begun. The knocking on the door upstairs seemed unnecessarily loud.

"He is in the library," the Ambassador explained. "Perhaps the traffic did not let him hear well."

The knocking continued, louder and louder, then ceased. Kanehira came running downstairs, in great agitation.

"There is no answer," he said in queer, clipped Berlitz English. "I think something wrong."

The three men leaped to their feet, and followed the valet at a run. At the head of the stairs they turned right and entered the corridor which ran the length of the east wing of the Embassy. All was dark and silent. They knocked. Again there was no answer.

An expression of apprehension and bewilderment crept across the face of Viscount Kondo. " I do not understand," he muttered.

" Let's break the door down," Acorn proposed. He shook the door-handle vigorously. It was firmly locked on the inside.

" Should we ? " the Secretary asked. Kondo nodded.

Acorn rushed at the door like a bull and struck it with his shoulder. It shook and the sudden boom echoed through the building. Again! There was a splintering this time. Again! It was giving. At the fourth charge the door tore loose from the lock and crashed inward. The three men, followed by the valet, entered the library. For a moment they stood uncertain, unable to see clearly in the dim light which filtered through the shutters from the street outside. Then, with a common impulse, they shrank back and stood huddled together in the doorway, staring incredulously at the spectacle of disaster.

The room bore evidence of a brief but desperate struggle. A chair lay on its side. In the fireplace was a broken glass. Another glass, inconsequentially empty, stood on the window-sill. A large picture of the Mikado over the fireplace hung at a crazy angle. A rare Turkoman rug in front of the hearth was rucked up in a heap. In the angle of the room between the window and the fireplace lay a body, crumpled and unconscious. It was the British Chargé. His face was scratched, there was a large bruise on his forehead, and he was breathing spasmodically.

But that was not the worst. In the Chargé's hand, still gripped loosely, was a heavy brass poker, and the end of the poker was strangely and horribly wet. For, across the floor, his head smashed in and stone-dead, lay the cousin of the Emperor of Japan.

The Ambassador uttered a hoarse cry and buried his face in his hands. The valet stood on the threshold, twisting his white-gloved hands foolishly, his face working and his eyes starting from his head as he looked on the master whom he had seen well and happy but a short half-hour before.

While the two older men stood back from the door, reluctant to enter the room, Acorn no longer hesitated. A familiar tingle of professional interest ran over him, his nostrils twitched slightly and his eyelids narrowed. The habit of years of legal practice came back to the Assistant Secretary. Once more he was the district attorney of his salad days at the law.

"It looks like a fight," he remarked and strode briskly into the room.

" Impossible ! " the Secretary of State protested.

Acorn stooped over the prostrate Prince, laid his ear against the dead man's breast, and listened.

" Dead ! " he observed, unnecessarily.

He looked at the unconscious Chargé. A familiar odour arose.

" Hm ! " commented Mr Acorn. " Gin ! "

He leaned over the British diplomat and scrutinized him closely.

" They have been fighting," he announced.

The Ambassador turned his haggard face reluctantly on the scene of disorder. " But it is not possible," Viscount Kondo insisted. " What shall we do ? "

" Do ? " demanded Acorn. " Send for the police. This looks mighty bad for Murray."

At the mention of the police the valet turned like a flash and ran downstairs.

" Do you think," quavered the Ambassador," —it is———? "

Acorn nodded. " It looks like a clear case," he said. " And I should like to hear how Murray can explain *this*." He pointed significantly at the bloodstained poker.

The Secretary of State stood clicking his tongue and cursing in a low and vehement voice.

II

TYLER TAKES CHARGE

DENNIS TYLER was strolling unconcernedly up Sixteenth Street. He was also perspiring profusely. There was a reason for that. It was the fag-end of a blistering August afternoon, and the Chief of the C.P.I. was wearing a ceremonial costume which included an impeccable morning-coat and a glistening high silk hat. In one hand he languidly toyed with a pair of light grey gloves and an ebony cane. Under his other arm was a large red morocco leather book, which proclaimed in flowing gilt script that it was an autograph album. The humorous gleam of his blue eyes, the uncompromising set of his jaw, and flare of his red hair proclaimed mischief of sorts.

Tyler, Chief of the Bureau of Current Political Intelligence of the Department of State, had been a thorn in the side of at least three Secretaries of State. He dressed too well to be popular with Congressmen. He knew too much to be dismissed from the service. He had too much initiative to be trusted in the field, and he ran his bureau without fear of his superiors or favours from politicians.

To the world at large his bureau—the C.P.I. of Departmental abbreviation—was just another Government publicity agency, engaged in preparing Press paragraphs and circulating newspaper clippings. Actually, it was known to its members as " the Brains of the Department " or " the Suicide Club," depending on how things were going. After Tyler's successful solution of the Howard murder, the San Pedro bombing, and the missing bond issue case, the Bureau had enjoyed public and official favour. But success is quickly forgotten. One of the Bureau's men in the field had just been imprisoned in a Central European fortress for knowing too much about a certain chemical factory in the Balkans, and three others had been ignominiously deported from a South American republic which prided itself on its ability to exasperate the Gringoes. So for some months " the Suicide Club " had been much in evidence, and only the jaunty and irrepressible optimism of Dennis Tyler saved the C.P.I. from relapsing into the placid and bovine acceptance of routine, which is the Nirvana of bureaucracy.

The Chief of the C.P.I. had needed all his optimism in facing the settled suspicion and opposition of Harrison Howard's successor, Mr James B. Acorn, whose honourable and lucrative career as attorney for the hydro-electric interests had *ipso facto* qualified him to act as a diplomat in negotiating with men who had devoted a lifetime to the service of their countries. Tyler's efforts to save this new Pharaoh " who knew not Moses " from the political bulrushes had created a good deal of bureaucratic tension, and only the steadfast support of the Secretary of State had saved Tyler from an official decapitation in the shape of an appointment as Consul-General at Leopoldville. To-day, however, he was cheerful. The exile to the Congo had been finally checkmated, and the C.P.I. was about to score on the Under Secretary, who had incautiously challenged Tyler's ability to get behind the official façade and learn the facts.

As he walked, Tyler was talking to himself. That is to say, he was talking in a clear, conversational tone. " This will teach the old fellow to try to put anything over on the C.P.I.," he observed. " The very idea! Just because a superannuated politician believes it his duty to put a cookie-pusher in his place, I have to suffer the torments of the damned."

As he rounded the corner at the Circle his pace quickened. " Hello, hello," he remarked, still conversationally, " what is up? "

The door of the Japanese Embassy swung violently

open, and a white-clad little figure scampered down the steps to the sidewalk and there stood, irresolutely, looking to right and left. As Tyler approached, the valet turned away and started briskly in the opposite direction.

Tyler lengthened his strides. " Here ! " he remarked, solicitously laying his hand on the shoulder of the hurrying Kanehira. " That's no way to act on a hot day. What's the trouble, eh ? "

The Japanese whirled round and stared at the bland young diplomat. " Police ! " he gasped. " I get police ! " and tried to break away. But Tyler's grip was firm.

" Now you don't mean to tell me you're looking for a policeman in Washington. Don't you know that all the police are out collecting evidence from bootleggers, preferably beer, in weather like this ? No, no, my man. That story doesn't ring true. You come on back to the Embassy with me and I'll attend to you. I'm a policeman of sorts. Tell me all your troubles."

The valet stared inscrutably at the tall intruder. " All ri'," he agreed. " You come with me."

They ascended the steps and entered the darkened building. On the doorstep Tyler paused and listened with undisguised delight to the abuse which was hurled at him by a brisk little old gentleman whom he recognized as a Secretary of State who was supposed to be lecturing to the natives of Darkest Ohio on world-peace and so forth.

" What in hell are *you* doing here ? " was the gist of the Secretary's comment.

Tyler smiled easily. " Why, revered sir and superior, I came to get an autograph from his Imperial Highness Prince Hojo. You see "—he continued hastily, to head off the glowering Mr Acorn, who with the Japanese Ambassador was flanking the Secretary—" the Assist-ant Secretary was so incautious as to make a small bet with the Chief of the C.P.I., ten dollars was the sum, sir, if you insist on knowing, that I couldn't guess where or why he was going over the week-end. We who are known as the Department's brains, sir, have our own little way of learning things, and so I called to see whether . . ."

" That's enough," snapped the old man. " You'll get no autograph from the Prince. He has been killed. It looks very bad for Bob Murray, Tyler, and there's the very devil to pay, the very devil to pay."

Tyler's actions were characteristic. " My God, how perfectly unnecessary ! " he exclaimed and turned and shut the front door.

"Why did you do that?" growled Acorn. "This is no time for fooling. The Ambassador here——"

Tyler groped through his vocabulary for an adequate epithet, gave it up, took off his hat, mopped his brow, laid his book, hat, stick, and gloves carefully upon a small table and turned to the Ambassador. Kondo looked old and shrunken, his mouth was trembling pitifully.

"Your Excellency," said Tyler earnestly, "this is a terrible calamity. May I not help you in some way? I am entirely at your service, sir."

Kondo bowed and smiled, pulling himself together with an obvious effort. "You are very kind, Mr Tyler," he said, "but I must request you gentlemen to leave. I must inform my Government and await their orders for my punishment. The Prince was in my care, under my roof, and there is nothing else for me to do."

"That is entirely true, Mr Ambassador," Tyler continued, "but for one thing. This may mean war, and we all know it. It means the absolute end of all our work, unless we can stop it. Let me try to help, sir."

"What do you propose to do, Mr Tyler?" The Ambassador's voice was tired and colourless. "It is a little late."

" Where's Murray? " demanded Tyler.

" Upstairs unconscious," the Secretary replied.

" And if I had any say in the matter he'd be on a patrol wagon," added Acorn. " He was still holding the weapon when we found him."

" Patrol wagon? " Tyler inquired. " That's the last place for Murray. I stopped the servant here from calling the police and it's very lucky for you all that I did, because in ten minutes the news would have been on the wires and the ends of the earth would have known that the British Chargé stood accused of attacking a Prince of the Imperial Family in the Japanese Embassy. War. Massacre. And all the rest of it."

" You can't suppress the truth," Acorn interjected fiercely.

" Oh, can't you? " Tyler's tone expressed earnest inquiry. " It's done in the best of circles every day. Besides, you haven't got the truth. You don't even know how or why Hojo was murdered. You suggest Murray did it. Did any of you see him do it? Probably not. We don't know the first thing about it. All we have is a probable murder and a probable murderer. We haven't got the truth."

" Tyler, you use too many words," the Secretary snarled. " What's your idea? "

Tyler turned swiftly on the old man. " Suppress it! Suppress everything! Mount guards all over the Embassy and see that nobody leaves. Cut the telephone wires and see that no word gets out. Stay here until Murray recovers consciousness and until we can get the truth out of him. Then, if you like, when we know the facts, tell them. Let Mr Acorn call his patrol wagon, let the Ambassador telegraph his Government, let us go out and build as many warships as we can, and get ready for war. But first let's know why."

The Secretary turned apologetically to the Ambassador. " Your Excellency," he begged, " I think Tyler is quite right. Is there any way we can help? Anything my Government can do is, of course, yours for the asking."

Kondo looked up with a quiet smile. " Mr Tyler *is* right," he agreed. " We should know more of this before we act." He went over to the wall, produced a key from his pocket, opened a small box, and disclosed a telephone. " Twelve men! " he said into the mouthpiece.

Acorn looked astonished. " Twelve men! " he exclaimed. The Ambassador had gone crazy, he decided. What did you do if an Ambassador went mad, anyhow? The Ambassador returned the receiver to its hook, closed and locked the box on the wall, and returned the key to his pocket. " We shall have guards in a moment," he remarked.

Tyler smiled to himself. So *that* secret was out. He had long known that certain Japanese subjects in Washington held themselves in readiness for duty at the Embassy's call, but he did not know until then that the Japanese intelligence service had organized them on so instantaneous a system. Valets, florists, caterers, chauffeurs, shopkeepers, all ready to respond at a moment's notice. A pretty neat trick, he thought, almost as good as the arrangement he had made at Tokio during the period of strain which had followed the A-A agreement of the year before.

" Now, Tyler," the Secretary snapped, " what's your next idea? We can't wait for ever."

" I suggest," Tyler remarked deferentially, " that we all sit down and rest until the reserves arrive. Perhaps while you and the Ambassador are talking, Mr Acorn can put me *au courant* with the situation."

Acorn glared suspiciously at the young diplomat. " Tailor's dummy," he thought. Then the desire to impart information overcame his loathing of Tyler's un-American ways.

" It's this way," he began, as the Ambassador and

the Secretary of State withdrew into the small reception room on the left of the entrance hall. " We were all downstairs, the Secretary and the Ambassador and I, while Murray was upstairs talking to the Prince. We heard some moving around up there, but we didn't know they were fighting until later. Then they sent up to tell the Prince that the Secretary was here, but couldn't get an answer. I thought that was rather suspicious. I was District Attorney myself once and I have a feeling for these things. So after a while we sent up again, and the servant came down and said they wouldn't answer. So we went upstairs and broke down the door and there we found them both, Prince Hojo as dead as a door-nail and the British Chargé unconscious. They'd been drinking, by the evidence, and the door was locked on the inside. Murray was holding the poker that had been used on the Prince. I'm afraid there's no doubt about it, even if Murray is a friend of yours. So we tied him up and decided to send for help."

" What's your theory, Mr Acorn ? " Tyler inquired, fascinated. In his head he ran over the priceless formula which years of diplomatic experience had taught him: " All political appointees are mistakes, but not necessarily fools."

"My theory?" Acorn beamed paternally. Tyler wasn't so bad a sort as he had thought. Had a fair head on him, in spite of his clothes. "I haven't got a theory. I leave that to the police. Give me the evidence there is upstairs and I'd send any man to the chair in any court of this land—bar millionaires and insanity," he added hastily.

Tyler considered. He had never lost confidence in the broad rule-of-thumb methods of American lawyers, and he knew that Acorn, for all his lack of diplomatic finesse, had been a first-class lawyer in a first-class city. The obvious conclusion from evidence sufficient to convict was not necessarily wrong.

"Did you search the house?" he inquired.

Acorn nodded. "Of course!" he answered. "We did that immediately. Everything was locked up. They have special locks on all doors and windows connected with the Holmes alarm. Only the Ambassador has the keys. Besides, there wasn't anybody else in the house. You could have heard a pin drop anywhere. It was—well, you can hear for yourself how quiet it is."

Tyler listened. He could hear the creak of the chairs where the two important diplomats were sitting and could even detect the slight asthmatic wheeze of the

Secretary's breathing. He could hear a fly buzzing excitedly against a window facing the garden at the back. He could hear the slow ticking creak of the woodwork on the upper floor as it adjusted itself to the minute contractions which were setting in as the sun slanted lower and the heat began to abate. It was as quiet as an empty house.

He turned to the Assistant Secretary. " It's curious that you didn't hear them fighting," he observed, " when you could have heard a pin drop."

Acorn turned this over in his mind. " That's so," he said, " but evidence is evidence and Murray must have done it."

" I'm not saying he didn't," Tyler argued patiently. " But I should like to know what you did hear."

" I heard——" Acorn began, and then stopped. " What was that ? "

A heartrending groan echoed through the building. " It must be Murray," Acorn commented. " We took him into the next room and tied him up. He's about ready to come to, I guess. What do you say to going up and seeing him ? "

" But what did you *hear* ? " Tyler insisted.

Acorn was impatient. " Nothing much," he announced. " The Jap went up with some drinks. I saw them myself and wished I had one. I heard him open the door and walk into the room and then I heard him close the door again and he came downstairs. That's all I heard until he went up and began knocking. Then he came down and said that he couldn't get an answer. The next time he went up and knocked, he came right down and said he thought there was trouble. Then we all went up and broke open the door. That's all. And now that Murray's coming to his senses I'm going up to hear what he has to say."

He arose, stretched himself, and started upstairs. Not since he had sent the Guicciardo gang to the chair for the murder of Tony Mello had he felt so happy. As he set his foot on the first stair, however, he stopped. A voice was calling.

" I say," the voice demanded, " I say, Poggles, old chap, what's the game? "

III

ON JAPANESE SOIL

IN a small anteroom on the upper floor of the
Japanese Embassy a tall young Englishman was
struggling with his bonds, jerking at the cords which
bound him hand and foot, and thinking unutterable
things of his predicament. He had a splitting headache.
He was trussed like a fowl. His cries for help were un-
answered. And he had only a large iron safe for company. The door was open and he could hear a hum of
voices from below the stair-well in the great entry
hall.

He stopped struggling, however, and relaxed.
Steps were mounting the stairs. A burly man stood
in the doorway. In the dim light Murray could not
recognize him. Then a hearty, impersonal voice
boomed at him. It reminded him of the time when in
his undergraduate days he had heard a famous " hang-
ing Judge " address the Oxford Union.

" Well, young man," said the voice, " why did
you do it ? "

" Do what ? "

" Ah-h-h——" He no longer recognized the voice,

having never witnessed a third degree. "Better tell me why."

Murray was British. Moreover, he was a diplomat. Finally, he recognized his interlocutor as the Assistant Secretary of State. He saw red. "My word, Mr Acorn," he shot back at the perspiring diplomat. "This is an outrage. I am his Britannic Majesty's representative and this is intolerable."

Acorn smiled grimly. "Prince Hojo was a cousin of the Emperor of Japan and his death *was* an outrage. Why did you kill him?"

The Chargé gasped. "Kill Hojo? What do you mean?" he stammered.

"You'd better tell me all about it, Murray. Why did you do it?"

The prostrate diplomat lost his temper. "It's none of your affair what I did or why. Will you kindly go straight to the devil!"

Acorn chuckled and turned away. "He's about ripe to confess, Tyler," he called out of the door. "Come on up. This is going to be good."

"Tyler! I say, Tyler!" The relief in Murray's voice was obvious. "Come up here and set me free."

Another patter of steps and Dennis Tyler appeared. "What's the trouble, old chap?" he inquired. "Has

due process of law been denied you or are they giving you the works?"

"Set me loose," the Englishman begged. "Your Assistant Secretary has gone stark staring mad and tells me I killed Prince Hojo."

"If you didn't, who did?" Tyler countered, stooping down and loosening the cords. "Watch your step," he whispered, "there's hell to pay and you're cast for the goat."

"Hey!" It was Acorn again. "What's the idea, letting him loose?"

"Mr Acorn"—Tyler's voice was edged with ice—"do you realize that you haven't got the slightest right to cross-examine Murray? He hasn't committed a shadow of a crime against anybody but the Japanese Government, no matter what you think he has done. I suggest we go downstairs and ask the Ambassador what he wants us to do. Bob"—he turned to the bewildered Chargé—"you had better stay here for the time being. Don't ask me why. Don't leave the room. Just trust good old Dennis and he'll see that the processes of justice don't drop upon you like a brick from a skyscraper."

Downstairs, the indignant Acorn and the worried C.P.I. man found the Secretary and the Ambassador sitting alone, old and listless, not even caring to speak.

While Acorn was clearing his throat in the manner which had been so effective in addressing a jury, Tyler nipped in ahead.

"Mr Ambassador," he explained, "I feel that I owe you an explanation. As I came to the Embassy, I found your servant hurrying for the police. Although it was really none of my business, I stopped him and brought him back with me. I didn't know what the trouble was then, but I knew that if it was serious enough to demand police attention, it was too serious to permit the Washington police to have anything to do with it. Moreover, now that I am here, by your courteous permission, Mr Acorn and I have recalled that we are on Japanese soil and that we can only act with your authority. The police may not enter here, and have neither the right nor the power to intervene. I believe, Mr Secretary," he added, "that I am correct in my assumption that there is no objection to my offering the Ambassador my personal services, if he cares to make use of them, but that no police could enter here without committing a grave affront against Japanese sovereignty."

The Secretary grunted. He turned to the Ambassador. "Of course, Tyler is right, Mr Ambassador. It's a damned annoying habit. Would you object to his trying his hand?"

The Ambassador considered carefully. " I should think that he might help, but I must naturally inform my Government at once."

Tyler leaped forward, tingling with eagerness. " Mr Ambassador," he pleaded, " let me handle this in my own way. Don't tell your Government yet, until we know what to tell them. It looks as though Murray had committed this crime, but until you hear what he has to say for himself you really have no right to treat him as though he were a criminal."

Acorn nodded. " Quite so," he remarked drily, " but that's no reason for untying him."

" I untied him," Tyler said, " because he can no longer escape. Your guards have arrived, have they not ? " he turned to the Ambassador.

The diplomat nodded. " They are outside now," he admitted.

" Call them in, where they won't attract attention," Tyler begged. " They'll do just as well inside as out and won't be nearly so conspicuous."

For answer the Ambassador arose and walked with faltering steps to the front door. There he struck a single deep booming note on a great gong that hung beside the entrance. He unlocked the great door and swung it open. In a moment twelve young Japanese

attired in motley costumes marched smartly in, in military formation, turned, dressed ranks and saluted the envoy of Japan. Tyler recognized two or three as valets, stewards, and the like whom he had seen in private residences or clubs. One, in a frock coat, was obviously a shop-owner, probably a curio-dealer. One in a crumpled, floury suit was a confectioner or caterer. Others were apparently of the student class, and the balance were in plain business suits. All, Tyler noticed, carried automatic pistols and bore themselves with the trained alertness of the well-drilled soldier. " Reservists," he concluded, "and a good-looking platoon of them."

The Ambassador addressed them in the sing-song, sibilant language of the Nipponese, and the men scattered, to the basement, to the garden, to the big reception room, wherever entry could be made. One was left on guard by the front door. Kondo turned with a polite little smile to Tyler. " Yess-s ? "

" Excellent, sir," Tyler agreed. " Now our prisoner can't escape and nobody can break in."

The Secretary snorted. " Tyler, *what's* the idea of all this foolery? We've got to have action, at once. This is no Harrison Howard case with months to work in and a fresh gardenia in your buttonhole every morning. This means war, for certain."

Tyler nodded coolly, " I know all that, my respected and impetuous superior. But we have time. We have until Monday morning."

" Monday morning? " the Secretary shouted. " Are you mad? "

" No, sir, only a simple American diplomat. If you'll allow me to explain my plan, I hope that the Ambassador will approve."

" Very well! "

The Ambassador said nothing. The current of the young American's energy seemed to sweep round him without moving him, like a stream around a boulder. His inner purpose had not been touched. He must inform the Emperor of this tragedy and then resign. Until then he could preserve his country's interests.

" Here's the scheme." Tyler, when he wanted, could be very brief. " No one knows that either you or Mr Acorn are in town, so no one will miss you. No one knows that the Prince was in this country, so no one will miss him. My wife is quite used to my staying out all night—er—at the Department, naturally. And she knows better than to inquire for me. Murray is a bachelor and is alone in the Embassy. His friends may miss him, but they won't worry about him. It won't be the first time on record that a British diplomat

has slipped away from his post over a week-end. Anybody that's looking for the Ambassador will find him here. They'll find him but they won't get away.

"That's why I had the men brought inside. Anybody that comes to the Embassy can be admitted, but they mustn't leave. All telephones but one should be disconnected and the Ambassador or some other reliable person, such as Mr Acorn or the Secretary, can watch that.

"We have until Monday morning to solve this matter and it's only Saturday afternoon. I propose that we keep the guards here until Monday morning and let no word of this leak out until then. If we turn people away, suspicion is sure to be aroused. But if we let them come in, we cannot only hold them, we may catch some one who knows something about it. At the same time, we can watch Murray. If he is guilty, he is more apt to betray himself if we let him wander round loose than if we keep him tied up. If he's innocent, we have no business interfering with him. Do you agree, Mr Ambassador?"

There was a pause. All three Americans gazed earnestly at the old Viscount. He said nothing and the seconds ticked themselves away into minutes. He sat, impassive, clutching the carved black woodwork on his armchair with two hands that looked like

yellow claws, his face sunken and lifeless in the dimly lighted room. He coughed lightly, to clear his throat.

" I agree, Mr Tyler," he said, at last. " It is a good plan. But there is one provision."

" Yes ? " The three Americans stared at the Oriental.

" This is Japanese soil. I shall administer Japanese justice on the man who has dared profane this Embassy and insult the Imperial Family. Mr Tyler can have his free hand now, but after midnight to-morrow, I shall take matters into my own hands, no matter how much or how little we know. Do you agree ? "

The Secretary turned a horrified countenance upon his subordinate. Acorn pursed his lips and looked wise. Tyler did not hesitate. " I agree, Mr Ambassador," he said. " You shall be the judge of this case and I shall abide by your verdict. If you choose to deal with the culprit, that is your affair. I shall have no further interest in the proceedings after midnight on Sunday."

There was a long sigh from the Secretary and a nervous little click of the tongue from Acorn. The three Americans withdrew, by a common impulse, to the hall, leaving the tragedy-stricken old Viscount still seated, impassive, in the shadows.

" Tyler," said the Secretary, in a strangled whisper, " if we ever get out of this place, I'll cheerfully kick

you down the front steps of the State Department.
And if you think I'm going to stay cooped up here for
a couple of days with a crazy young Britisher and a
Japanese whose hands are itching to shed blood, you're
a Chinaman. I'm going!"

The old man jerked angrily away and started for
the door. Before he could lay his hand on the knob,
however, the guard darted forward, pistol drawn, and
barred the way.

"Hey," the Secretary ejaculated furiously, "what's
the idea? Do you know who I am? I'm the Secretary
of State." He waited for the guard to shrink and
shrivel. He did neither. He simply stood, quiet,
pistol levelled, and waited.

"Here, Tyler," the Secretary demanded, "this is
your doing. Tell him to stand aside."

Tyler addressed a few words of hesitant Japanese
to the guard. He smiled politely but made no move.
He had his orders. Tyler shrugged his shoulders. "You
see, dear old Excellency," he observed soothingly,
" it's an old Russian custom. The police-trap. A very
neat idea. You see how well it works. Anybody can
get in. Nobody can get out. Of course, if you ask the
Ambassador to let you go, he'll probably agree, but then,
he'll cable Tokio, slice poor old Murray into mincemeat,

and generally raise hell with the peace of nations. Trust one, sir, who has never failed you except at nine o'clock in the morning—which is an ungodly hour to go to work, anyhow. I was relying on your soothing influence to keep the Ambassador from running amuck. Be a sport, sir, if you'll pardon the suggestion."

The Secretary frowned. "For two pins I'd ask Kondo as a personal favour to me to cut *you* to mince-meat. But, damn it, you're right, Tyler, though you don't know the difference between a protocol and a convention. I'll stay, if only to see you suffer."

Acorn grinned. "I'll stay, too," he rumbled. "I wouldn't miss this for a barrel of monkeys."

Tyler sighed with relief. "The C.P.I. couldn't ask for more loyal support," he assured them. "I will now, gentlemen, first roll up my sleeves to show you that I have nothing concealed in my apparel and then will proceed to remove the rabbit from——"

He stopped. There had been a ring at the doorbell, sharp, imperious, impatient, such as a woman gives. The trap was about to claim its first victim. Before the men could shrink out of sight or the guards conceal their weapons, the peal was repeated. Who could be calling at the Japanese Embassy at this hour, when every one knew that the Embassy had been closed for the summer?

IV

THE FEMININE ELEMENT

"HELLO, Dennis," a girl's voice sang out. "Is Bob Murray here?"

It was Peggy Lawrence, the *débutante* daughter of the Senior Senator from Massachusetts, looking cool and sweet as a primrose in her simple little tennis costume (by Patou). Behind her, in flannels, lounged the easy, feline figure of Francis Urquhart, Press Adviser of the Japanese Embassy ("which," Tyler had often observed, "is a damned roundabout way of saying publicity agent").

Tyler, whom the girl had spied from the threshold just as he was about to slip unobtrusively into the living-room, hastily assumed his most languid and enervated air.

"Hello!" he drawled, "isn't the heat *ghastly*? God bless my spats, but I can't conceive of playing tennis on a day like this. How *do* you do it? And how do you happen to blow in *here*, of all unlikely places?"

Urquhart followed Peggy into the hall and the guard deftly swung the door to, behind him. The trap was sprung. The Press Adviser was a tall man, in his late

thirties, with a small close-clipped black moustache, and hair that was greying at the temples. His lips were just a little too full and red and his manner just a little too smooth and graceful to seem altogether agreeable, but, Tyler reflected, he was a smart fellow for all that and had the run of all the best clubs.

" The Ambassador wanted me to call in this afternoon," he explained. " I got a telegram from the Secretary this morning, and Peggy ran across Murray this morning at Rauscher's and they made some sort of dinner-date for this evening. So we put in an afternoon at the Montgomery, mixed doubles, and here we are. What's up? "

Tyler closed his eyes for a moment and thought rapidly. It was all just a little pat and unconvincing and he didn't like the concluding question. Just the same, that didn't mean that it wasn't the truth. " The first rule of successful crime detection," he had often, and amid hoots of derision, informed his subordinates, " is to suspect the most unlikely person. Detective stories always do, and they are always right." He hastily concocted an elaborate plot, in which Urquhart had murdered the Prince and thrown the blame on Murray in order to win the hand of Peggy Lawrence. It was a pity they had spent the afternoon at the

Montgomery Club. Otherwise, everything fitted. Bob
Murray and Peggy had been suspiciously chummy
during the past season and "Dame Rumour"—as Tyler
elegantly expressed it—had linked their names more than
once. Urquhart had been dancing attendance on Peggy
for a couple of years. He was an ageing bachelor;
Peggy had been his last hope. Jealousy! Intrigue!
Murder! What a pity about the club and the tennis——

"Dennis," begged Peggy incisively, "please close
your mouth and run and find Bob for me. He said
he'd be ready at five and it's long past that now."

The Chief of the C.P.I. had not been happily married
for a year to allow himself to be bullied by a *débutante*.
"Come! come! my dear child," he remarked aus-
terely. "That's no way to speak to a statesman.
Murray is detained by urgent business and won't be
ready for some time. You go and talk with the Assistant Secretary, who will doubtless tell you about how
he sent Joe Pegliacci and his gang to the chair for the
murder of somebody or other, while Frank and I go
upstairs and have a little conference."

Peggy pouted. "I suppose that's another word for
drink."

Tyler was scandalized. "God bless you, child," he
exclaimed, "I wish it *were* a drink! Run along now.

You'll find Acorn in the big reception room. I've really got to take Urquhart upstairs at once."

Peggy walked diffidently to the door, which stood slightly ajar. She opened it and walked in, to find herself confronting three old gentlemen who certainly did not appear delighted to see her. She went without hesitation to the Secretary. "How do you do, Uncle Stephen?" she remarked. "I thought Father said you were in Ohio. How do you do, Mr Ambassador. And Mr Acorn—I hope I'm not interrupting a conference."

The Secretary glared at her. "Peggy," he snapped, "I always told your mother she ought to spank you more. You shouldn't have come here. Acorn," he added, "will you take my niece out in the garden and keep her out of mischief? As I was saying, your Excellency——"

Peggy gave an imitation shiver, as she walked out into the garden through the French window which Acorn had opened with perspiring clumsiness. "It's cold in there," she said.

Tyler turned to the mystified Urquhart. "Come on upstairs," he said, "there's big doings here to-day."

The Press Adviser followed the young diplomat with excitement. "Good Lord, Dennis," he inquired, "what's up? Something on the A-A order?"

" Why do you ask that ? " Dennis rejoined abruptly.
" What's the Anglo-American Agreement got to do
with you ? "

His interlocutor was unabashed. " Just putting two
and two together, old-timer," he answered easily.
" Murray's here, the Secstate's here and his Excellency
is here. And you tell me that there's big doings.
Looks like another line-up in the Pacific to me."

Tyler turned—they had reached the second floor—
and watched his man closely. " And it looks like
battle, murder, and sudden death to me," he announced.

" Murder, eh ? " the other laughed. " Who's getting
away with it now ? "

" That's what I'd like to know," Tyler admitted.
" But really, my dear old compatriot and Press Agent,
just take a look in that library and tell me if you don't
think it's enough to make my monocle skip a beat."
He flung open the door of the room where the dead
Prince lay and again glued his eyes on Urquhart's
sallow features.

" My God ! " the wretched Press Agent gulped. " My
God ! My God ! Here, let me out of here, quick."
Whereupon, the man backed hastily out of the death-
chamber and leaned against the wall of the passage,

battling with nausea. " Who—er—who is it? " he managed to ask at last.

" Who *is* it! " Tyler almost shrieked. " It's Prince Hojo of Japan. That's who it is, and he was killed less than an hour ago and probably by the British Chargé d'Affaires. That's all! And what do you know about that? "

Tyler's question was purely rhetorical and colloquial, but Urquhart took it literally. " What in hell should *I* know about it? " he snarled. " I've been playing tennis all afternoon with Peggy at the club. Why, I didn't even know the Prince was in the country! Last we heard, he was in Portugal. What *should* I know about it? " He was almost hysterical.

" Steady, my distracted old Press Agent," Tyler soothed him. " I just told you that Bob Murray killed him, according to the evidence, though the poor fellow stoutly denies all knowledge of said crime, which I understand is conventional under the circumstances." Urquhart was rapidly recovering his self-control, while Tyler prattled on.

" Here's the situation. We've got till midnight to-morrow to discover if, how and why Murray did it. Until then, we're not to let a soul know that anything's wrong. It might make a little unpleasantness, you see.

The Ambassador is quite capable of assisting Murray into the other world when the time limit is up. So you see there's a chance for all sorts of trouble. You Press Agents will have your hands full, I can tell you, when the Emperor's cousin is murdered by the British Chargé and the British Chargé is decapitated by the Japanese Ambassador right here in Washington. God help the code-clerks and the navies when the story breaks. Now I want you to help me. You know the ropes here. Why in the name of God and hot weather should Bob Murray bash in the head of Prince Hojo? I ask you."

Urquhart had pulled himself together, not aware that Tyler had been talking in a tone which could carry into the next room, where Murray sat, his aching head in his feverish hands, the taste of sulphur in his mouth, his throat dry and his eyes stinging, as he tried to appreciate his position. Urquhart smiled at Tyler.

" That's only too easy, I'm afraid. You may not know that there's always been a streak of homicidal mania in the Murray family. The founder of the house was an earl who did rather unpleasant things to his tenants in the Elizabethan era. His grandfather was court-martialled after the Indian Mutiny for undue

severity towards the natives and his father died in the Sudan leading a cavalry charge at Omdurman. They're really a family of soldiers. Murray did rather well in the War, I remember, got the D.S.O. and the Military Cross. There's a wild streak in that blood, Tyler. Funny thing about homicidal mania is that they come to, afterwards, as though they'd been drunk and don't remember a thing about it. Not a very useful thing in a diplomat, is it?"

"Or in a husband," thought Tyler. "So that's how it is," he continued out loud. He was surprised at the thoroughness of the documentation. Urquhart had omitted no essential statement, save the tale which was current in London clubs which assigned Bob Murray's paternity not to the dashing if bloodthirsty gentleman who had died in a Dervish rush at Omdurman, but to an equally dashing individual with royal blood in his veins. In which case homicidal mania was unlikely as an hereditary attribute. Of course, the gossip might be wrong, though Tyler had long ago had occasion to comment that there was an uncanny accuracy about such rumours and that gossip was much more likely to lead you to the truth through uncharitable short-cuts than any amount of authenticated evidence.

"Where's Murray now?" Urquhart demanded
eagerly.

"Up in one of these rooms," Tyler told him. "And I
should gather that he's about ready to be examined before
a tribunal consisting of our respective excellencies."

Peggy had walked around the garden three times,
with the cumbrous Acorn at her side, before she
realized that something was wrong. The garden was
charming, beyond any question, but when a man
doesn't know the difference between a tea-rose and a
gardenia, he is apt to blunder with a woman.

Acorn blundered. The truth was, he was lonely.
His wife was fat and refused to live in or near Washington in the summer, which was very wise of her. Acorn
was the sort of man who takes his stenographer to an
hotel, wishes he dared hold her hand, dances with her,
too close and too energetically, and then scolds the
girl in the morning for mistakes in dictation. Peggy
was an attractive girl, *petite*, well formed, with the blue
eyes, fair hair, and pink cheeks of seaboard New
England. Also, she had lived with her father in
official Washington for two years and was used to
flirting with fleshy politicians who came to discuss the
tariff and the returns from the Western counties in
the last gubernatorial election.

" Isn't this garden marvellous? " she inquired, automatically suiting the banality to her companion, with the instinctive tact of a politician's daughter.

Acorn smiled meaningly at her, a mixture of wistfulness and paternalism which reminded her of a St Bernard eyeing a dog-biscuit. " It's a nice garden," the Assistant Secretary of State agreed, heartily.

Peggy said nothing. Inside her pretty little head thoughts were racing along, " like motors on the Baltimore pike," she thought to herself. They went by so fast she could no more reduce them to words than she could have worked out in mental addition the sum of their licence numbers as the cars of her simile rushed past her. Something *terrible* must have happened, she concluded.

" Don't you think we ought to go indoors? " she suggested. " Bob Murray promised to take me to dinner."

Acorn gulped and mopped his brow. " I don't think Murray will be able to take you," he grumbled. " He's got an important reason for staying here."

" Mr Acorn! " Peggy's voice cut the hot still air of the garden like a stiletto. " What's the matter? "

" Why—why—what do you mean? " He tried to look innocent.

She looked at him steadily. " You know perfectly well what I mean," she insisted. " Tell me! Why does Uncle Stephen look so worried and why do you have to take me out in the garden when it's much cooler indoors? What's the trouble? "

Before Acorn could answer they were interrupted by a call from the house. The Secretary of State had come to the window. " Acorn," he said, " come on back at once. Peggy, you stay where you are till we call you. Acorn, Murray's coming downstairs now and we'll see what he has to say."

Peggy's eyes sparkled angrily and her bosom rose and fell swiftly. She looked as fresh and thorny as a wild rose, one of those wild roses which clamber on the crumbling stone walls of a fog-swept New England pasture on the shores of Cape Ann. " All right," she answered, " I'll wait." She waited till the French window was slammed to, then crossed the garden quickly and pressed her ear close against the crack of the window. She heard a murmur of voices, low, tense, and ominous, with a clear English voice singing out in a sort of cadenced question-and-answer game. Her heart was pounding furiously. " What *are* they doing? " she asked herself.

UNDER CROSS-EXAMINATION

DENNIS TYLER was soliloquizing. It was, as his subordinates had often pointed out, one of his more irritating habits. The Chief of the C.P.I. preferred to term it "thinking on one's feet," but it remained his habit, in moments of exasperation, bewilderment, or anxiety, to wander round with a vacant look in his eye and a polysyllabic stream of honeyed objurgation flowing from his lips. On this occasion he was awaiting the signal from his chief to bring down Lord Robert Murray for a cross-examination to be conducted by Urquhart and Acorn, in the presence of the Ambassador and the Secretary.

He had found a little leeway in the hall, where his mutterings would not disturb the two elder statesmen, who, aided by highly technical objections from the Assistant Secretary of State, were discussing the appropriate method of questioning the British Chargé.

"And all"—Dennis observed—"just to discover whether the blistering idiot murdered the cousin of the Emperor of Japan. A perfectly simple matter. All you really need do is go right up to Murray and say, 'Murray, old horse, did you or did you not murder Prince Hojo

with a brass poker, or did you use some other blunt instrument, such as Mr Acorn?' And Murray would answer me without batting an eyelash,' Tyler, I cannot tell an untruth. I did not kill the Prince Hojo with a brass poker and I will thank you to remember that I am *not* an old horse.' But God bless the shades of Blackstone, it has to be done in legal mumbo-jumbo. Old Kondo has to put on a black cap. My revered but none too scrupulous chief divides himself by twelve and prepares to bring in a jury's verdict with a recommendation to mercy. Acorn is busy looking for the moving-picture cameras and microphones of the time he sent Joe Pappagoosis and fifteen innocent bootleggers to the chair on the charge of putting dynamite in the baby's milk, and I have acted as turnkey, bailiff, and counsel for the defence. It's all about as intelligent as an Act of Congress to regulate the automatic chewing-gum apparatus on the island of Guam and not nearly as funny."

He paused a moment, closed his mouth twice firmly, blinked his eyes, swallowed once, and resumed his pacing. " And the trouble with it all is that whichever way it turns out there's going to be simply rapturous hell to pay in about thirty hours. Japan gets mortally offended at the murder of her Prince, as well she may. The agreement goes up in smoke and Hong-Kong and

Manila do too, or I miss my guess. Let's see who stands to win in this shake-up. Our dear old hairy friends do, of course, and the big Pan-Asiatic gang do too. We lose, the Limeys lose, and the highly susceptible Japanese lose their shirts for the greater glory of somebody. It's simply too perfectly horrible to happen and, as the girl said to the soldier, 'Oh, 'Arry, it 'as 'appened!'"

" Tyler! " the Old Man's bark punctured the bubble of his babbling as a well-aimed anti-aircraft shell punctures a captive balloon.

" Yes, Mr Secretary? " Tyler's voice was meek.

" Tyler," snapped the Secretary, " try not to look like an undertaker's assistant and bring Murray down. We want to talk to him."

" Yes, Mr Secretary."

Tyler about-faced smartly, strode from the room with military precision, and went up the stairs. He knocked at the door of the small green anteroom where the luckless Chargé was cooling his heels and wishing his head would stop aching. " The prisoner," remarked Dennis in hollow tones, " wore a bright green necktie and ate a hearty breakfast."

The Chargé grinned ruefully. " See here, Dennis," he begged, " what's up? I gather I've committed a murder or such."

Tyler gazed at him with a bright knowing look. " If that were only all," he murmured. " Tell me, Murray, old horse, did you or did you not murder Prince Hojo with a brass poker, or other blunt instrument? "

" Hojo? " Murray gasped. " You don't really mean to tell me that I'm seriously accused of doing in poor old Poggles? "

" No one else could have done it, Bob," Tyler argued. " So far as we can see you were the last man with the Prince and you were found beside the body."

Murray gasped. " My God! " he cried. " How ghastly! Dennis, I swear I never touched him! Why, I *couldn't* have—he was one of my oldest friends."

" You can tell all that to the jury," Tyler informed him, officially. " Shake a leg now, old diplomaniac, and prepare to give an account of yourself."

The two youngsters came down the stairs arm in arm, but before reaching the door of the great reception room where the others were waiting Tyler detached himself and walked ahead. " The prisoner, your Excellencies," he announced, not without dignity.

" Sit down! " The Secretary's order was abrupt. He turned to the Ambassador. " Shall we proceed, your Excellency? "

Viscount Kondo nodded. He was seated behind

a table in the corner. Upon the table lay his ceremonial sword in its sharkskin sheath. Flanking him on
either side were the Secretary and Acorn. The whole
resembled a slightly malicious caricature of the law.
Facing the three older men, on the opposite side of the
table, sat Tyler, Urquhart, and Murray, the latter in the
middle. Acorn cleared his throat. He wanted to hear
somebody call, " Order in the Court ! " It didn't seem
right. The Assistant Secretary was thinking of that big
meeting when he and Joe Choate had got the Massachusetts Central crowd to settle out of court with the
B.O. & I., for a million dollars and attorneys' fees. The
Ambassador was not thinking. He was waiting.

" Well, young man," Acorn suggested ponderously,
" what have you to say for yourself ? "

" Lord Robert," announced Tyler, with great suavity,
" desires to tell your Excellencies everything. He relies
upon the integrity and—er—the integrity of the gentlemen here present to protect his interests as the accused
from abuse. Suppose, Murray, that you tell us exactly
what happened."

" At half-past three," the Chargé d'Affaires began
abruptly, " I came to the Embassy. I had known the
Prince quite well at Oxford. In fact, I always called
him Poggles. This may explain a little the relationship

there was between us. I never thought of him as a member of the Japanese Imperial family but simply as a friend, and I knew that he wanted to see me before the formal meeting began. I wanted to see him. I was ushered upstairs, after I had paid my respects to the Ambassador, by the servant of the Prince, good old Kanehira. As soon as the Prince saw me, he said, ' Let's have a talk before the big guns arrive and how about a little drink? ' I said ' Righto! ' He said, ' Kanehira, bring two big Uncle Sams! ' ' Uncle Sams? ' I asked. ' Yes,' he said, ' Uncle Sams—lemon juice, plenty of sugar and sodawater, entirely non-alcoholic, except for a good slug of gin! ' That was the sort of chap Poggles—I mean the Prince—was. We talked of one of two things, while waiting for the drinks, a bit about the War, and he was telling me a few things he'd picked up in Madrid and Lisbon. One of them was a blonde, if your Excellencies wish to know what we really discussed, and the Prince said that he thought blondes were vastly overrated, and I told him they were infinitely superior to brunettes in every way but brains, and then finally the drinks came, and I can tell you they were a long time coming.

" The Prince clicked glasses with me and said, ' A short life and a gay one and no headaches! ' It was an

old Oxford toast, which we always drank bottoms-up to. So we downed it. After that we talked a bit, and then the next thing I knew I was lying tied in that room with the safe. I had a splitting headache and I gathered that somebody had killed the Prince. That's all I know about it."

The three old men said nothing. Urquhart smiled nervously. "Your Excellency," he suggested, "may I ask a few questions? It may help."

The Ambassador's eyelids flicked once in assent.

Urquhart smiled and stroked his moustache with his forefinger, first one side and the other.

"Is it true that several of your relatives and ancestors in the direct line have been put in asylums?"

The young Englishman began to look troubled for the first time.

"Yes," he replied, brusquely.

"What was the cause of their commitment, Lord Robert?" Urquhart concluded, with an air of pardonable triumph.

"Homicidal mania." The words were low and indistinct. A gulf seemed to have opened at the Chargé's feet, and a hand seemed to have reached out of the grave to thrust him into it. Insanity!

Acorn took up the chase. The question-and-answer

game had aroused the demon that lurks in the heart of every trial lawyer.

" Lord Robert," he began, " you said a little while ago that you did not regard Prince Hojo as a member of the Imperial family but simply as a friend. By that, I presume, that you would feel no differently about his death than you would over the death of any other college friend of yours. That so? "

" I regard my friends very highly, Mr Acorn," Murray rejoined, in an even, cold voice.

" Just so. Just so. You were talking about women, about white women, with the Prince, were you not? "

" Excuse me, sir, about blondes and brunettes."

" Yes, about blondes and brunettes. The Prince was telling you of his successes with blondes and brunettes in Spain. You British feel pretty strongly about white women and men of other—er——" Acorn coughed in embarrassment and looked at the Ambassador.

" You mean, Mr Acorn," Viscount Kondo said, " that the British, like the Americans, have a strong race prejudice? "

" Exactly, your Honour—your Excellency. Tell me, Lord Robert, did you feel entirely comfortable when Prince Hojo told you that he had picked up some white women in Spain? "

" I told him," the Englishman replied, " that if that was all he had picked up in Spain he was lucky. I felt no sense of distaste, if that's what you mean."

" But you argued with him. I suggest, Lord Robert," Acorn continued, in his more restrained court-room manner, " that you had a bitter argument with him, that you resented his attentions to white women, that you felt no sense of awe of his rank, but regarded him as a simple individual, that you saw suddenly, gleaming across the room, a brass poker. I suggest that when you saw that poker, you lost control of yourself, that old—er—ancestral tendencies asserted themselves. I suggest that you seized said poker and did then and there maliciously and feloniously assault the deceased with said poker and did kill him with it, and that then only, owing to the heat, the drink you admit you had taken and the single blow which your victim was able to give you, collapsed on the floor in the state of stupor in which we found you, still holding the bloodstained poker. Is not this what really happened, Lord Robert? "

Acorn stopped, mopped his brow and looked round instinctively for the glass of water which he used in court-room pleadings.

" Perfect rot! " Murray's comment was withering. He felt a sense of greater security and ease, which altered

swiftly to bewilderment and alarm as Tyler suddenly turned on him and began his questioning anew.

" Bob," remarked the Chief of the C.P.I., with distinct coolness, " you must remember that you stand accused of a very serious crime by very convincing evidence. Mr Acorn's summary of the situation cannot be characterized as rot. It is an excellent presentation of motives and acts which would probably secure your conviction before any jury in the world. We all know of the tendency to homicidal mania in your family and we all know that it would exonerate you, morally at least, in our eyes if you confessed the crime. The circumstances indicate that it was absolutely impossible for anyone but you to have killed the Prince. The door was locked on the inside. No one could have entered or left. The Prince lay dead and you lay unconscious beside him, holding the instrument with which he had been killed. I am your friend, Bob," Tyler continued in a less formal manner, " and you, as a diplomat, know what this tragedy must mean to the peace of the world, if it is not explained. By the kindness of the Ambassador, we have until midnight to-morrow to find out the truth. Until then no word is to get out. We might solve all this right now if you admitted that you might have committed the deed while temporarily insane."

Tyler's line of argument had its purpose. "If," the Chief of the C.P.I. had told himself, "Bob Murray takes advantage of a loophole to crawl out of this mess, he's guilty. But if he sticks by his guns, he's innocent and nothing can make me believe otherwise." Would Murray take the 'easy way' and lean upon the plea of insanity as a means of escape or would he play the game to the end? Until Tyler was absolutely convinced, beyond the slightest shadow of doubt, that Lord Robert was innocent, he did not dare set in motion the bold plans which were forming themselves in his resourceful brain.

Murray's face expressed bewilderment and rising indignation. "I most certainly will not confess to a deed I did not commit," he exclaimed hotly. "If you care to declare me insane and commit me to a lunatic asylum, go ahead. I'll submit in order to let you have a plausible explanation until this blows over. But I did not do this and I'll never say I did, either here or in the presence of lunacy commissioners. That's final. I'll do my best to help you clear up this mystery and I'll obey orders, but you can't make me say that I killed poor Poggles, just to smooth things over."

Acorn turned eagerly to the Secretary and whispered in his ear. The old man shook his head, gloomily, but remained silent.

" May I suggest——" Tyler began, when there was a sudden loud peal on the bell. The six men fell silent and listened. There was the sound of the opening of the front door and then a loud, nasal voice boomed through the quiet of the empty house.

" You can tell Mr Urquhart," the voice proclaimed, " that Bill Strong of the Amalgamated Press wants to see him."

Five pairs of eyes turned accusingly on Urquhart.

The Press Adviser of the Embassy blushed. " My God! " he murmured. " It's the Amalgamated Press man. I saw him early this morning at the club and told him to drop in here late this afternoon."

Tyler looked at him, with amused interest. " Very well, my poor old Press Agent," he said, " what an extraordinary coincidence! This is your funeral. You've got to handle it."

" I'll send him away," said Urquhart hastily.

" You forget," Tyler remarked blandly, " that nobody can leave the Embassy. Now we're locked in with the biggest news story since the Sarajevo murders and the most hard-boiled reporter in the entire North American continent."

c

THE INEVITABLE REPORTER

BILL STRONG delivered his message to the door-man at the Embassy, then stood back and waited for action. Strong lived up to his name. Six foot two in his stockinged feet, with a Secret Service jaw, a red face with beetling black eyebrows, small piggy eyes, iron-grey hair, and two hundred pounds of avoirdupois, he had often been mistaken for a minor official at the Department of Justice. Actually, he was the most dangerous newspaper man in the Capital, an old war-horse who had covered the Russo-Japanese unpleasant-ness, the Balkan Wars, and the Eastern Front with the German Armies. He had drunk his way up from police reporter to city hall man on the New York *Star*, had been Albany man for the *Globe*, Washington man for the *Herald*; and when Munsey sold the *Herald* Strong had formed his own syndicate and had broken more big news stories than any other man in the Congres-sional Press Galleries. He it was who had discovered the existence of a soon-to-be-famous electrical horse, he had turned up the Oil Scandals, he had put Nica-ragua on the front page, and had invented a series of

nicknames for several Cabinet Members which had followed them into the history books and, worse still, into private life. It was he who had called Tyler's Chief " Stuttering Steve," and he was a free lance upon whom no one paper could bring pressure, who could neither be bought, cajoled, nor mystified into obsequious compliance.

Bill Strong smelled news. It was there in every accent of the old house, with its drawn blinds, in the ticking of the big clock in the hall, in the very complacency of the big bronze Buddha who sat on a black marble pedestal at the foot of the stairs. There was news in the tense Japanese who stood watch by the door through which Strong had come, news in the subdued murmur of voices which came from the reception room. News!

Suddenly the door of the reception room swung open and the Press Adviser strode out to greet him.

" Hullo, Frank," said Strong. " What's doin'? "

Urquhart was obviously ill at ease. " Sorry, Bill. When I saw you this morning I thought I might have a story for you. But now there's nothing doing. Absolutely nothing. Not a thing," he added, with emphasis.

" Yeah? " Strong was obviously incredulous. " How

about my seeing the Ambassador? I'd like to get something from him. What's he doing here anyhow? Thought he was up in New England."

" The Ambassador! " Urquhart tried to simulate surprise. " The Ambassador isn't here. That's only some friends."

" Only friends, eh? Listen——"

Strong cupped his hand to his ear, ignored Urquhart and stared fixedly past the preoccupied Buddha toward the half-open door. A moment later he was rewarded by a voice.

" God bless us each and all, Mr Secretary, I say the thing to do with him is——"

Strong's lackadaisical attitude dropped instantly. He turned on Urquhart and grasped him by the arm in a grip that made the poor Press Adviser wince.

" The Secretary? Why, he's in Pittsburgh! Hell, man, you mustn't try to put anything over on me. What's this all about, hey? "

Urquhart stepped in front of the reporter. " Sorry, Bill, you can't go in there. They're having some sort of a conference. Something to do with the immigration question. It really isn't anything."

Strong laughed brutally. " Immigration! I'll have to look into this." He shouldered Urquhart aside and

lunged forward to the door, flung it open and took a look inside. He jumped back as though he had been shot.

" What's up ? " he demanded tensely. " You might as well tell me. You don't get Murray, Acorn, Tyler, Stuttering Steve, and your Chief in town on a day like this unless it's big medicine. Come across, boy. You can't keep anything from little Bill. And, say, what's wrong with the Ambassador ? I've only seen him look like that once before and that was at the Battle of Mukden, more than twenty years ago. What is it ? A war ? "

Urquhart was reduced to helpless confusion. " Sorry, Bill, but I can't tell you."

Strong smiled good-humouredly. " Can't tell me, can't you ? That's a hot one ! Well, that's what I'm here for. I'll just sit down and wait until there's something you can tell me."

To his surprise the Press Adviser seemed greatly relieved. " That's fine. You just sit here and wait. I'll speak with the Ambassador."

Urquhart was received in stony silence by the five men in the reception room. " I'm sorry, your Excellency," he apologized, " but he would stay !"

Acorn cleared his throat. " Stay, will he ? That's

a good thing. I'd like to see him get out now. He'd find himself full of lead if he tried it. Not that that would be a bad thing for the Administration."

"May I make a suggestion?" Tyler inquired plaintively. "It's all very depressing to have the black sheep of the Fourth Estate quartered upon us by compulsion, but at least we know where he is. I wouldn't trust Bill Strong outside for a million dollars. He knows news. Now that he's here we can keep him under our eyes. I suggest that Mr Acorn go and try to persuade him to leave."

Mr Acorn was somewhat mystified and said so.

"You see," Tyler explained, "nothing makes a newspaper man feel more at home than to be shown he is not wanted. If Mr Acorn shows Strong that he is *persona non grata*, wild horses could not tear him away from this Embassy. Then I have a little plan for keeping him from making trouble while we conduct this investigation."

Acorn strode out into the hall and glared officially at the carefree and unembarrassed Mr Strong.

"Afraid there's nothing here for you to-day, Strong," he remarked offensively. "If you see me after the regular Press Conference on Monday, I'll give you the story."

Strong beamed. " That's O.K. with me. I think I'll stick round for a while. The Ambassador may have something for me a little later."

Mr Acorn grew red in the face. " Don't try any monkey-tricks round here, young man "—he and Strong were actually the same age—" or the United States Government can make things damned unpleasant for you."

Strong still beamed. " Such as a little more wiretapping and nasty questions about my income-tax? Thanks. They tried all that on me when I turned up the oil stink. It all makes good copy for my papers. What is all the excitement about, Mr Acorn? All I want is the story."

" You won't get any story out of me," stormed Acorn. " You newspaper men think this town is run for your benefit. Well, it's not! "

" Yes, and when I tell you the people whose benefit it *is* run for you call me a muck-raker. No, I'll stick round until I can see the Ambassador. He's a squareshooter and this, by the way, is *his* Embassy."

Acorn turned with dignity and walked away. " Guess that did the trick! " he informed his colleagues. " Now, Tyler, it's your ante! "

Tyler demurred. " I'm afraid my head isn't strong

enough," he said. " This is where Murray makes himself useful. If the Ambassador will permit, I suggest that Murray takes the over-confident Mr Strong to the Press room in the basement and offers him a drink of Embassy liquor. Bill Strong has only one weakness and that's drink. My idea is for Murray to take him downstairs, make him drunk, and keep him drunk. So long as there is plenty of good liquor, Strong will be as happy as a baby, won't make trouble for anybody, and won't get curious about what's upstairs."

" My cellar is at your disposal. Kanehira will give you what you require," the Ambassador agreed, and turned away.

" Keep your end up," Tyler whispered to Murray as the Englishman walked out into the hall.

Murray went casually up to the stubborn reporter and whispered in his ear. The result was miraculous. " Bet your life I would! " Strong exclaimed delightedly.

A few minutes later they were seated facing one another across a little table in a basement room. Between them stood a couple of bottles of Burgundy and some wine-glasses. Through a little window high in the wall the fragrance of grass and flowers drifted in from the garden. The frigidaire was chilling the

White Rock and making ice for the whiskies-and-soda which were to follow when the wine was exhausted.

" Cheerio ! " said Murray.

" Glad to see you on board ! " agreed Strong.

They drained their glasses and poured themselves a fresh drink.

" Cheerio ! "

" Glad to see you on board ! "

The drinking bout had begun.

" Say, Lord Robert," inquired Strong, with the usual diffidence which bedevils an American reporter when he interviews an English official. "What's all the trouble ? "

" Hanged if I know," Murray informed him, with careless candour. " I got a wire from the F.O. to show up here to-day. The Ambassador and your Secretary of State are having some sort of talk and the F.O. expect me to keep tabs on it. God knows when they'll have anything to say. I'm thirsty ! Let's open the other bottle, what ? "

" Say, that's a great idea ! "

Peggy Lawrence was pacing restlessly up and down the garden. She was getting tired of being kept waiting by Robert Murray. The trouble was that Englishmen expected women to wait on them hand and foot. Well, she wouldn't wait a minute longer.

At that moment she was electrified by hearing a man's voice, issuing apparently from a bed of hollyhocks. But he wasn't speaking. He was singing. She listened.

> " Oh the sages sing of an ancient king
> These many years ago,
> He ruled his land with an iron hand
> But his mind was weak and low ! "

Curious, the girl walked closer and peered through the hollyhocks. Behind them she saw was a window. Inside she could see Murray. In his hand he held a glass of red wine. Facing him was another man, also with a glass of wine. Bob Murray was drinking in a cellar with a low rowdy individual. She heard the recreant's voice cut across the rollicking ballad which the other man had initiated. " See here, old chap," the cool English voice said, " why is it that you American newspaper men can't drink without singing foul songs ? "

Peggy was in no mood to appreciate the resentful shock which had made Bill Strong resolve that he would behave in such a way as to show this damned superior Englishman that an American newspaper man could be just as damned well bred as anybody else.

Unaware that a deft bit of alcoholic diplomacy had

saved her lovely ears from one of the more outrageous of the " men only " ballads and that Murray's future might depend upon his ability to put Bill Strong under the table, Peggy sought relief for her mortification in flight. She walked briskly back to the French windows which led to the reception room, pulled one of them open, and walked in upon the group of diplomats.

" I don't think I'll wait for Robert any longer, Uncle Stephen," she told the Secretary. " You'll excuse me, won't you, Mr Ambassador? Good-bye, Mr Acorn. Dennis, you look *too* hot in those lovely clothes. Thanks for the tennis, Frank."

She started for the hall. In a moment she would be trying to leave. In a moment the guard would stop her and an indignant *débutante* would be added to the complexities of Dennis Tyler's already intolerably intricate problem. He moved rapidly.

" I wouldn't go just yet, Peggy," he said soothingly. " Bob will be free almost any minute now and he can explain things to you. Come with me and I'll show you the Ambassador's Hokusais."

Before the bewildered and angry girl could resist he took her firmly by the hand and led her into the small reception room.

" This," he said suavely, " is one of Hokusai's most

famous prints. It looks like a cross-section of a huckle-berry pie with whipped cream on top, but is known as *The Wave* and is familiar to all students of that famous master of the colour-print!"

"Dennis!" said Peggy desperately. "Take me home at once. I can't bear it here. Please be a lamb and take me!"

"Now this," continued Dennis, " is in an altogether different vein. You will note the unusual perspective employed in the treatment of Fujiyama, Peggy, and you will observe—*don't scream, Peggy*—that the use of brown and grey as a *leit-motif*—*Bob is in terrible danger*—God bless us all, what's all this?"

Peggy had not screamed. She had burst into scorn-ful laughter.

PEGGY DEMANDS AN EXPLANATION

DENNIS thought that he understood women, because he had married one. Nevertheless, he felt at a distinct loss in dealing with Peggy Lawrence. What could you do with a girl who shrieked with laughter when you told her that her lover was in danger? And he had done it very discreetly, too, he flattered himself.

The girl stopped laughing abruptly. It was as though some one had removed the needle from a gramophone record. "Good-bye, Dennis," she said and turned away. In a moment she was in the hall and had started for the front door. Unobtrusively, but with shadowy swiftness, the guard stepped forward between her and the door-handle. In a moment more there would have been the dreaded collision, but Peggy started back impulsively.

"Tell me, Dennis," she begged, "what *is* all this about?"

Tyler wiped his forehead with relief. "My dear Peggy," he declared in a fatherly manner, "that was just what I was trying to do when you started giggling.

Giggling," he added, " is a most objectionable habit. I have experienced grave difficulty in curing Cynthia of it and now, it appears, I shall have to begin with you."

Peggy smiled at his fatuous face. " Don't be a fool," she advised lightly. " Tell me why that man at the door doesn't want me to go. It's almost as though I was a prisoner. First Mr Acorn takes me out in the garden and flirts with me."

" Naughty! Naughty! " was Tyler's comment, " but it takes two to flirt."

" Not with Mr Acorn! "

" Great oaks, remember, Peggy! "

She sobered immediately. " Something is wrong, I know it is. Please tell me, Dennis. Why did Mr Acorn take me out in the garden and leave me there and why do you try to show me a lot of silly pictures? Why is everything so queer? "

" Come out into the garden, Peg," half-quoted Dennis, " and I'll tell you everything."

Peggy brightened perceptibly at the prospect.

" I ought to go home," she demurred.

" Are they expecting you? " Tyler asked.

" Oh, no! They think I'm motoring out to Gibson Island for the week-end, but the party's off and that's

why Robert and I——" She broke off abruptly and bit her lip.

The garden was close and hot, although the sun had set, and there was a touch of thunder in the still, moist air. Even so, it was less oppressive than the shuttered house, with the three old men muttering in the reception room and the general air of furtive desolation.

" Now, Peggy," Tyler announced authoritatively, as he sat beside her on an ornamental marble bench in a tiny arbour by the wall which fenced off the alley which ran round two sides of the Embassy grounds. " Bob Murray is in terrible danger ! "

" Ha, ha ! " said Peggy bitterly. " Danger of *delirium tremens*. It's no use, Dennis," she continued hurriedly before he could interrupt. " I saw Bob, and all he's doing is drinking in the cellar."

" But you don't understand," expostulated the Chief of the C.P.I., as men have always protested to women. " Bob is drinking only because it is his duty."

" He's a slave to his duty," Peggy cuttingly retaliated. " England expects every diplomat to do his drinking."

" That's clever," Tyler replied, " I read it myself in the Washington *Post* this morning. Just forget about yourself, Peggy, and pull yourself together. What if

Bob has kept you waiting? The real question is, Will you help him? He's in real danger. He's in danger of his life."

Peggy's lip curled. "Why?" was all she asked.

"He's suspected of murder," Dennis explained, sounding less and less plausible to himself. Was the whole thing a gigantic nightmare? Would he awaken in a few minutes to discover that he was sleeping on the wrong side or had eaten too much curry at the club?

"Nonsense!"

Peggy got up determinedly. "Dennis," she said, "Bob has a good friend in you, but you can't lie at all convincingly."

"Can't lie!" Dennis was insulted. "Good heavens, my dear child, can't you see if I were trying to lie I could think of fifty explanations more convincing than the truth! Can't lie? That's the first time anybody has dared suggest I am deficient in the elements of diplomatic training. Can't lie, indeed? See here, Peggy Lawrence, you won't believe me, you'll have to believe somebody. You can't leave this Embassy. I can't leave it. Nobody can leave it. Somebody's been killed and everybody thinks Bob did it. Unless you believe me, you'll just make trouble and get in the way like any fool woman."

Peggy smiled. In spite of her age she felt immeasurably older and more experienced than Dennis, who was at least twelve years her elder. "Is your definition of a fool woman one who won't believe you?"

Tyler growled. "For two depreciated roubles, Peggy, I'd pick you up and lay you at the feet of the Secretary of State. I'll give you one more chance. You may not believe me, but you'll have to believe Bob."

Leaving her bright-eyed and excited, Dennis jumped up and ran to the other end of the garden. Pushing aside the hollyhocks, he tapped on the little window which ventilated the Embassy Press room. All was silent. He listened. There was no light inside, and though the afterglow was still bright in the western sky, there was not enough daylight to see clearly in the room. Tyler was about to light a match when he felt a tap on his shoulder. Stifling a desire to scream, he turned and faced Murray, tall and nonchalant in his flannels, with a strong aroma of vintage Burgundy about him, and a happy note of exhilaration in his manner.

"All sereno," the Chargé assured him. "Strong just curled up for a little shut-eye. After he had had a bottle of wine and the best part of a bottle of whisky

he said he felt tired. Before then, he told me the story of his life, tried to explain the Russian tactics at the battle of Mukden and read me a long lecture on how the Allies really lost the War. After that he showed me how the Cossacks dance and then wrapped his shoes up in his coat, to make a pillow for himself, and went sound asleep. He's safe for a little while, at least."

" Robert," begged Tyler, " for heaven's sake go over and talk to Peggy Lawrence. She's insulted at your lack of consideration for her. Do you realize the crime you've committed. You have kept a *débutante* waiting."

Murray was all penitence. " I say," he said, " that's so, is it? Bad for her prestige to be cold-shouldered. We'll have to have a few *pourparlers* and an exchange of notes and so forth."

" Well? " Peggy was icy and ominous, as the two men approached her, with obvious uneasiness on Tyler's part and the foolhardiness of ignorance on Murray's.

" Sorry." Murray was casual. " It was no end good of you to wait for me like this. The fact is that I'm in a ghastly mess and I'm hoping you'll help me out of it."

" Robert Murray," expostulated Peggy indignantly, " you've been drinking when you should have been attending to me."

" And jolly good wine, too, I can assure you. The Embassy does itself proud in that line."

Dennis coughed meaningly. " I'm a bit out of place in a lovers' quarrel," he informed them and strolled away. Neither of them paid any attention.

Peggy tried to look severe but could not. After all, he had a right to drink. He simply had no right to look so happy and healthy, especially if he were actually in danger.

" Robert, what is Dennis talking about ? " she asked softly. " He is such a tease that I can't believe him. Are you really in trouble ? "

He looked deep into her questioning eyes. " Yes," he said slowly. " I'm in the dickens of a mess. I came here early this afternoon to see poor old Poggles— that's Prince Hojo of Japan, you know—whom I used to know at Oxford. We had a drink or so and a little talk, and when I woke up Poggles had been killed and they told me I had done it."

" Oh, Bob! You didn't do it. You couldn't have done it ! "

He looked at her again, for a long minute, and then

laughed harshly. " I could swear I didn't, old girl, but—I—don't—know——"

" Nonsense. I know. And I know you never could have hurt anybody."

" Shake ! "

The Englishman extended a large brown paw and took her slim brown hand. Their hands met in a grip which seemed to last an eternity and which sent little electric tingles through them.

" Thanks ! " he said brokenly. " But I don't think anybody else will agree with you ! "

" Dennis ! " Peggy's voice was imperative. " Come here ! "

He came at a trot. " I'm afraid," he said, " we're going to have a storm. It feels like thunder to me."

" Never mind the weather. What do *you* think of all this ? "

Dennis temporized. " The question is not so much whether I believe him guilty as whether I can prove him innocent. We've got till to-morrow night to turn the trick, and we haven't got anything to work with. Why, even in the Howard investigation I had the dim-witted police to sharpen my brain on, but here I haven't got a thing. The three of us have simply got to prove that Bob couldn't have done it. How can

we? You'll say Bob didn't do it. Good! Unfortunately, he was the only person who could have done it. You'll say he's not the sort of man who kills a friend. Unfortunately, Frank Urquhart will say that he is just that sort, on account of a family failing. You'll say that the drinks were obviously drugged. Good! I ask you how you're going to have an autopsy or police investigation of any sort without provoking the sort of publicity which must be avoided? Why, we don't even dare call in a doctor to help us learn what happened. You see, Peggy, this is a case to be handled by intuition. We've got to decide 'who' did it and 'why,' we can let 'how' run until later. Whom do you suspect? The valet? He had been the Prince's bodyguard for twenty years and was devoted to him. Besides, he was upstairs on only three brief occasions. Once when he served the drinks, which may not have been drugged at all. Once when he went up to announce that the Secretary had arrived. Once when he went up the second time to try to call the Prince. On each occasion every sound he made was distinctly heard by the Ambassador and Mr Acorn. The Secretary arrived after the deed was done. So did I. So did you and Urquhart, for that matter. Then there is the possibility of some one coming in from the outside.

How could he have done so without making a noise or attracting attention and how could he have escaped? The shutters were bolted on the inside, although the windows were open and the door was fastened on the inside by a spring lock. The moment after Acorn had finished tying up Robert, they all made a tour and examined all doors and windows. Nobody could have got in or out. Everything was fast. On the other hand, Robert *was* in the room with the Prince and showed signs of having had some sort of a struggle. The Prince was dead and Robert was lying unconscious, holding the brass poker which had been used by the criminal. Plenty of men have gone to the chair on less than that. We say, ' Robert couldn't have done it.' The others will simply say, ' Robert did it.' "

Peggy thought for a long time. Then she asked a curiously irrelevant question. " How was the Prince dressed? " she inquired.

" Good old Peggy! " Tyler exclaimed. " Trust a woman to ask for fashion notes! Why," he added, " I think you have a germ of an idea there."

Murray considered carefully. Like most men he was remarkably unobservant of the details which one took for granted. Clothes were among such details. If they

were inappropriate he noticed them, otherwise not. " Let me see," he reflected, " he was wearing the usual sort of clothes for this weather. Light-coloured suit of sorts."

" Tie? " Peggy inquired.

" Ox-blood," Murray replied quickly. " I remember pulling his leg about it. He said he wore it to remind him of the days when he was an Oxford blood, before he had to go in for all this royal rot."

" Stiff collar? "

" Of course not! Who besides Dennis would be ass enough to wear a stiff collar in weather like this? Poggles had on some sort of a soft shirt."

" Was it a light blue shirt, with collar attached? " she asked.

" Peggy! " Tyler interposed, " you've been looking in the forbidden room! "

" Was he wearing white silk socks and white buckskin shoes? " she continued triumphantly.

" Yes," Murray agreed, " I think he was, now that you say so."

" Were you standing or sitting when you drank and talked—before the Secretary came, I mean? "

" Sitting, of course. Why stand when you can sit? " Tyler was quite positive on this point.

" Sitting, naturally," Robert corroborated.

" And the shutters were locked? " Peggy continued.

" He told you they were," Tyler reminded her.

" So the room was quite dark? "

" Yes—but what has all this got to do with it? "

Murray's jaw dropped, for Dennis Tyler leaped to his feet, pirouetted gracefully, went up to Peggy, and, before she could object, kissed her warmly on both cheeks.

" I say! " Murray objected. " What is the idea? "

Tyler laughed, pirouetted, and laughed again. " Out of the mouths of babes and so forth. You see, Bob, Peggy has just elicited from you the information that you and the Prince were dressed almost identically and that it was so dark in the room that one of you might easily have been mistaken for the other."

" You mean? "

" I mean that the fellow that did for poor old Hojo might really have intended to kill you. Have you been doing anything to anybody to justify your murder? Think carefully. Count ten before answering and then don't."

" But I don't see that that brings us any nearer to the solution of the question," Murray objected.

Tyler's mood of elation collapsed in ruins at his

feet. " That's true," he said. " It doesn't. So we're just where we were before."

" Not quite," said Peggy, and her voice had a curious singing quality in it, a sound like trumpets being blown upon wind-swept battlements. " You've got me working for Bob now."

" That also," said the Chief of the C.P.I., " is absolutely true, and you've only got twenty-four hours to do it in."

" What shall our first move be? " Bob inquired, blissfully.

" I know what mine will be," Dennis assured him. " I shall rout out that valet and get him to cook me some rice and give me a bottle of Burgundy and a couch. I'm going to have some food and sleep. I've done enough thinking on an empty stomach."

" Did you say ' stomach '? " the Chargé inquired ironically.

The two watched Tyler as he walked fastidiously down the garden path and back to the house. The Chargé d'Affaires turned to the daughter of the Senator from Massachusetts. " He's a stout fellow," he said, and he kissed her without more ado.

VIII

INTERMEZZO

THE clouds had gathered black and close to earth, pressing a mask of hot moist air against the earth's sleeping face. Little gusts of wind at the street-corners whipped the dust into momentary swirls and scrolls which danced faint arabesques beneath the glare of the arc-lights. Over by Anacostia there was a growl and grumble of distant thunder. From time to time the clouds gleamed like copper in the glow of a far-off flash of lightning. Up in the Maryland hills the mercy of the rain had been loosed, but here in the marshy pocket by the Potomac the Capital lay, restless and stifled, as in an ether dream, a dream shot through by stabs of light and punctuated by the uneasy thunder.

Suddenly a door banged to with a crack like a pistol-shot. A blast of cold air swept down the avenue, carrying before it a wrack of dust and blowing papers, like jetsam hurled up a beach by an advancing wave. A roar and rushing like wings swept over the Embassy. The growl of the thunder was louder now and the flashes of lightning were making patterns on the

clouds. But still there was no rain. The earth seemed to ache and strain for the cool slash of the storm, cruelly withheld like a sacrificial sword poised over the city.

Now there was a slow patter, like small footsteps. A drop fell hissing to the pavement, large, warm, dust-laden—another drop. They were falling slowly by twos and threes. The wind whipped up the dust and where the drops fell little spurts of dust made rings. Then, over the house-tops, came a slow steady clash as a curtain of rain brushed nearer. There was a blinding blue-white flash and an explosion of thunder, a moment's pause, and then a choking, blinding cold downpour, as straight and fierce as an Indian's hair. The sky was pouring water. Water swirled and choked in the littered gutters and the parched drains; it spread inkily in pock-marked puddles; it chattered at the eaves.

The rain slashed down, tearing the leaves from trees and shrubs, leaving them plastered to the pavements. The street-lights beat bluely on the smooth ice-black asphalt. From time to time a little white foaming line marched across the deserted Circle, as the wind whipped the rain forward. The rain fell harder and harder, in a fury of foaming intensity.

The thunder and the flashes came closer together. The lightning was dancing now on every side, the clouds still reflecting and concealing it in a wild hide-and-seek, so one could never quite know where the last flash had been, except when, for a instant, a white-hot tree of blue fire veined the black night in splendid agony, as a bolt struck. The thunder burst and roared, like guns, like guns firing at sea. Now together, now singly, now far away, now terribly close.

The old Embassy shook and strained beneath the lash of the storm. Timbers groaned and creaked. From somewhere came a sudden drip-drip-drip. A shutter slammed somewhere back and forth, as the freakish gusts swept first one way and then veered. In the garden, the roses had been beaten to earth and the hollyhocks were splayed and battered. Only the musky-smelling box hedges quickened and thrust eagerly against the downpour.

There was a single blinding flash as a tree in front of the Embassy was struck and a crack as though a bomb had been set off. The noise awakened Dennis; every one else in the Embassy had been unable to sleep. He, however, fortified by a bottle of Moulin-à-Vent and some excellent *suki-yaki* that Kanehira had conjured from the basement kitchen for him, had been

sleeping the sleep of the unjust, which, as he had often observed, is much sounder than that of the just.

For some moments he did not quite realize where he was. Used to wakening in places he had never consciously seen before, however, he soon recollected that the damnably uncomfortable couch on which he lay was in the upper hall of the Embassy. He groaned and listened resentfully to the clamour of the storm. Downstairs a faint murmur of voices drifted up to him, and he gathered that Peggy, Urquhart, and the three old men were keeping vigil. A glance at his luminous wrist-watch told him that it was just after midnight. A brief lull in the storm brought him a cheery drift of sound from the basement, the voice of Bill Strong raised in the musical rendering of some ballad for the delectation of Murray, he gathered from the few words he caught before the wind and the rain and the thunder blotted journalism into reputable silence.

" Damn all Oriental cookery! " he groaned, as a sudden painful emptiness made him realize that rice, though undeniably filling, lasts but a moment in the belly of the Anglo-Saxon carnivore. Well, there was no use trying to sleep while that row was going on.

He would explore a little. He didn't care to go downstairs. In the first place he was conscious of not looking his best. His suit was badly creased, his collar awry, and he was beginning to need a shave.

"And besides," he commented inaudibly, "the notion of sitting in silence while three diplomatic fossils exchange reminiscences of the Congress of Vienna, and a baby like Peggy and a flannelled fool like Frank Urquhart talk tennis, is too horrible for words."

He rose and paced slowly along toward the corridor which led to the rooms in the wing, past the door of the library where Prince Hojo lay dead. He moved noiselessly, having removed his shoes when he first lay down on the sofa "to think things over." Suddenly he paused. A familiar Fourth-of-July sort of fragrance drifted delicately to his sensitive nostrils. "Now who," he asked himself, "is burning punk at this ungodly hour?"

He peered into the little anteroom which held the Embassy safe and where Murray had been imprisoned after the discovery of the crime. All was dark. He walked quietly as a cat to the room at the far end of the corridor, a largish and moderately useless sort of upstairs sitting-room, with a fireplace in the centre

wall and windows opening on to both the garden and the street. All was dark there, too. The scent of the joss-sticks was stronger now. A bright flash of lightning illuminated the room, despite the closed shutters. It was empty, save for the furniture which crouched shrouded in its summer dust-sheets.

Whatever it was, it must be in the library. Who, however, would go into that room where lay the dead man? Possibly the Ambassador, out of respect to the dead, had ordered some vigil by the corpse. Possibly some propitiatory ceremony was prescribed by custom. One never knew what would be considered proper in a case like this.

The library door stood slightly ajar. The shattered lock still dangled from the splintered panel. The reek of incense was overpowering. Tyler pushed the door gently. It swung wide, creaking loudly on its twisted hinges. Tyler caught a glimpse of a white-clad figure kneeling on the floor in front of the silent thing which lay stretched out on the couch between the two windows. The room was thick with the smoke of joss and a score of tiny glowing eyes shone redly through the gloom from the smouldering sticks. The intruder had but a moment to glimpse this. The instant the door had opened, the kneeling figure leaped to its feet and

rushed at him wildly. In a flash of lightning, Tyler saw a small dark face, convulsed with grief and the fury of surprise.

" Why, it's Kanehira," he said, soothingly. " Sorry. Thought there was something wrong."

The valet halted abruptly and bowed politely. " Yess! " Kanehira hissed. " Yess! Yess! "

Closing the door behind him, Tyler tiptoed away. He felt like a beast to have intruded on the loyal little valet's vigil by his dead master. He knew how loyalty was bred into the bone and sinew of the Japanese and had an inkling of the crushing loss which a devoted servant like Kanehira must feel for the prince he had followed and served for twenty years. When he tried to add to that the special veneration which a loyal Japanese must feel for a member of the Imperial family, Tyler leaned over the abyss of Eastern character, so difficult for the Westerner to fathom, so simple for the Easterner to know. Tyler knew, by experience, that death by suicide for a Japanese in Kanehira's situation was simply as logical and natural as it would be for himself to wear a black tie. Tyler felt a fury of disgust for his intrusion on this naked grief. It is never pleasant to see another's soul stripped bare. As he tiptoed moodily back to his

couch, he was haunted by the memory of the expression he had seen on Kanehira's face—grief-struck, horror-struck, frightened. Yes, Kanehira had been frightened. That access of fury came only with fear.

"Now why," Tyler murmured, "should poor old Kanehira be frightened by the innocent old Chief of the C.P.I. ? "

He buried his face in his hands and plunged in thought. Thought eluded him, spiralling mockingly away into blackness, leading him back by irrelevant and stupid images, luring him into depths of emptiness. It was no use. The lightning flickered less frequently and the thunder was far away. The rain had ceased to be a downpour and no longer worked its grey traceries on the pavement. Tyler put his legs up on the couch again and continued to pursue the little demon of intelligent ratiocination down the empty corridors of his brain. Fear? Why fear? Why——

A few minutes later a gentle snore was the only sign that the Chief of the Bureau of Current Political Intelligence of the Department of State was engaged in solving the greatest political crime which had ever tainted the Western hemisphere—bar, Tyler would have added, the appointment of William Jennings Bryan as Secretary of State.

D

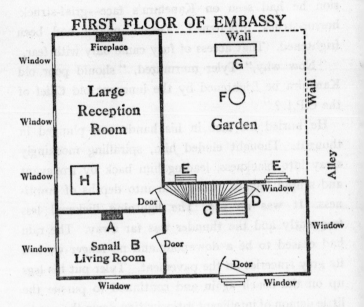

FIRST FLOOR OF EMBASSY

Wall

Fireplace

Window

Large Reception Room

Window

Garden

G

F

Window

H

E

E

Door

Window

C

D

Small Living Room

A

B

Door

Window

Door

Window

Window

Wall

Alley

A. Fireplace.

B. Where the Ambassador, the Secretary of State, and the Under-Secretary heard the knocks.

C. Bronze statue of Buddha.

D. Door to basement.

E. Steps leading down from garden to basement.

F. Fountain.

G. Arbour.

H. Table with telephone.

PART II

PART II

I

THE BOOTLEGGER'S MEMORY

SUNDAY morning dawned hot and clear. The storm had relieved the humidity, but the sun beat down strong and steady from the blue-grey of the August sky. Over the closed and shuttered Embassy hung a pall of gloom shot through by flashes of irritation from tense nerves and weary brains.

With the exception of Tyler all had spent a sleepless night. Peggy alone appeared miraculously neat and fresh, having sat up for hours talking with Murray. The three older men presented an ominous and sobering spectacle—clothes crumpled and eyes reddened from lack of sleep. They were sitting as Tyler had left them, round the table in the great reception room, with a litter of cigar-ash and a sweetish reek of stale whisky to show how they had watched through the night.

The Secretary had a baleful glare in his eye when Dennis sauntered into the room, his hair tousled, badly in need of a shave, and his once immaculate clothes looking as though he had been wrestling with wild bulls. The Chief of the C.P.I. tried to appear jaunty,

but catching the eye of his superior—Acorn was frankly drowsing and the Ambassador was staring straight in front of himself with blank inscrutable eyes—he thought better of it.

"Good morning, sir," was all he said.

"'Morning," his superior grumbled. "What are you going to do now?"

"Have some breakfast, Excellency," said Tyler eagerly, "and then set to work." He rubbed his hands efficiently.

"Hm!" was the Secretary's only response.

With the respectful celerity of a man who has by inadvertence strolled into the wrong wash-room, Tyler withdrew. Once he was out of sight in the small reception room, he mopped his forehead. He caught sight of Peggy, sitting listlessly in an armchair, staring at the floor.

"Well," he ventured, more cheerfully, "how about some breakfast?"

She smiled. "Good morning. Have a good sleep? No breakfast for anybody but tea or whisky. Kanehira ran out of provisions and the Ambassador won't let anyone near the telephone or I'd call Rauscher's to send over a square meal. You," she added bitterly, "had the last food in the Embassy last

night, while everybody else was worrying about poor Robert."

" What? No breakfast? " Tyler's voice was really distressed. " This is very bad management. Nothing but tea and whisky, eh? Well, for once in my life I'll take tea. Have some? "

Peggy answered hollowly. " I've had five cups already and I still feel empty."

" Try some whisky, then," Tyler suggested.

" I have," she admitted, " and I wish I hadn't."

" Take a little more and try to get some sleep," he counselled.

" Dennis,"—there was a world of reproach in her voice—" do you think that I could be so heartless at a time like this? "

He shrugged his shoulders and tiptoed from that room. His usual ebullient spirits were beginning to slacken beneath the doom which brooded over the deserted house. The weary Japanese standing guard at the front door, the garden littered and trampled by the rain, the despondent girl, the three hard-eyed old men with their drone of talk, and that strange bloody thing upstairs which had a few hours ago been Prince Hojo of the Imperial Family, suddenly obtruded the sense of quickening drama upon the blue-eyed and

sanguine young diplomat. He pulled himself together roughly.

" See here, Dennis, you fool," he told himself—*sotto voce*, as was his custom—" you mustn't let this get you. It's only a problem you've got to solve before midnight, not the second act of a melodrama. It's all perfectly simple. Just find out who murdered Prince Hojo in the next eighteen hours and you'll have a happy ending on your hands. Just——"

" Shut up, you silly ass!" His meditations were interrupted by Lord Robert, pink-cheeked and clear-eyed. " Do you want the whole Embassy to know what you're thinking?"

" Oh, it's you, Bob!" Tyler exclaimed. " I'm famishing. Come on and have a spot of whisky with me. I need something."

" Right!"

The two young men slipped down the service stairs, walked along the short corridor which led to the kitchen and sat down by a porcelain-topped table in the somewhat forbidding presence of a large electric refrigerator, but in the soothing company of a bottle of pre-War Haig and Haig.

" Am I alone and unobserved? I am!" quoted Tyler, and poured himself a stiff eye-opener.

"Tyler," said the Chargé earnestly, "this is a damned bad business. You've got to pull me out of it. Last night everything seemed mad enough and queer enough to have been just a dream, but this morning I've come to the conclusion that I'll have to do a bunk."

"You can't," Tyler assured him. "Every exit is guarded and the men have orders to shoot. Besides, if you clear out, your guilt is established. You've simply got to face the music. You've got me and you've got Peggy working for you, and we've got eighteen hours. After that—well, I won't let you down."

"Damn it all," the young Englishman threw aside his pretence of reserve with a rush. "You're no end decent, Dennis, but what can we do? Peggy's a dear sweet girl, but all she says is that of course I couldn't have done it and that she'll tell the Ambassador so. I can see as well as anyone how guilty I must look, but I swear that I didn't do it and know no more about it than you do. I don't see anything for it but to pretend I went mad and let them lock me up. I'm hanged if I'll let anyone do me in or persuade me to do the gentlemanly with a revolver just because there's not the time to iron things out."

Tyler took a long reflective drink of whisky-and-soda. The hot light from the garden filtered through the shrubs about the high-set window and bathed the kitchen in a green and aqueous light.

"Here's what I say," he said at length. "There's no food in the house and everybody's going to lose their patience in this damned heat. Peggy and I are for you to the end. Bill Strong's just an accident. He doesn't count one way or another——"

"You're jolly right, he doesn't—not where drinks are concerned," Murray interjected. "Do you know that he's had the best part of two bottles of that whisky since yesterday and I expect him to call for a third any moment?"

"The dirty dog! We'll attend to him later. To continue—the Secretary's not against you and if it weren't for the fact that old Acorn had once in his misguided and lucrative career been a prosecuting attorney we could count him out too. He may make trouble, but I can hold him up. The Ambassador is set. He'll stay put until midnight. I never knew him to go back on his word in the slightest particular. The thing for us to find is, who is working against you."

"Since you've only left out Urquhart and Kanehira that should be simple," Murray commented wearily.

"No, my lad, I know when I'm for it. You'll be no nearer a solution by to-night than you are now. Until then, eat and be merry."

"Now that's exactly where you're wrong," Dennis assured him hotly. "That's the whole trouble with your whole service, Murray, since we're on the subject. You've taken a position on practically every point you can and then are surprised when you run into trouble. You've forgotten old Asquith and the great principle of 'wait and see.' Give this business a little time to cook. Give hunger, whisky, and hot weather a chance and you'll get action of some sort."

The Englishman sighed. "I hope you're right," he said. "But I feel in my bones that I'm for it this time."

"Now that that's settled," Tyler continued briskly, "what shall we do about Bill Strong? We simply can't go on wasting good pre-War liquor on a mere newspaperman. It's not done. It's scandalous, particularly when it's not our liquor. Wars have been fought for less than that."

"Strong!" Murray's voice was vibrant. "He's a card! You'd never think that fellow had brains. Spent all the evening talking about the Yoshiwara at Tokio and the tactics of the battle of Mukden—that and drinking. I kept him from singing."

" You wait here," counselled Tyler. " I'll fix Strong.
I'll call up Joe O'Connor and tell him to bring round a
case of the latest sample of the noble experiment. If
Washington's best bootlegger can't make Bill Strong
feel that he's Senator Brookhart at the Century Club,
I'll pay for the funeral myself."

Tyler walked briskly upstairs, wondering mildly
where Urquhart was, and addressed the Ambassador.
" Mr Ambassador," he inquired, " have I your permission to telephone for a man to bring some more
whisky? It is part of my—er—plan of detection," he
added.

The Ambassador shook his head.

Tyler was undaunted. " Will you, Mr Ambassador,
telephone to Joe O'Connor and ask him to deliver a
case of whisky here at once? He always works alone
and once he's here we can use him to keep Mr Strong
from becoming too inquisitive. Please, your Excellency, this is really important. Strong is drinking all
your whisky and it's not bad enough to keep him from
making trouble."

The Ambassador thought for a long moment.
" Very well, Mr Tyler," he replied at last. " What is
the number?"

Tyler told him and stood waiting anxiously while he

put through the call. When the message had been delivered, he sighed with relief. "Thank you, your Excellency. That will hold him for a while."

At that moment the door swung open and Strong himself appeared, very red as to face, dangerous as to demeanour. "See here," he said thickly, "I want to interview Pince—beg pardon—Prince Hojo. Want to see him at once. Most important!"

Four pairs of eyes turned on him swiftly. "What do you know about Prince Hojo?" Tyler asked him casually, slipping between him and the door.

Strong laughed. "It takes a lot to fool Bill Strong," he admitted. "I found some papers in Frank Urquhart's office downstairs, if you want to know," he added. "Just said the Prince had been here and had conferred with Murray and the Secretary. Looked like a regular Press release. 'T any rate, I want to talk with the Prince."

"You can't," Tyler said softly.

"Why not?" Strong's surprise was the incomprehending amazement of an American journalist who is denied an interview. "Why can't I? All I want to ask him is how he likes America and does he think American girls are the prettiest in the world. His being here's the story, and I want to give it to my paper."

" You can't have the story," Tyler told him.

" Yeah ? " Strong smiled. " I've got the story right now and I'm going home to write it."

" No, you're not," Tyler informed him. " And you haven't got the story. See here, Bill, old man, stick round and you'll get something worth having. Joe O'Connor's on the way with some more liquor and we'll see that you get the news before anybody else does."

Strong smiled generously. That was better. That was the way he should be treated. It had looked for a minute as though they were holding out on him. " O.K. by me ! " he remarked. " Just a moment while I flash my office——" and he reached for the telephone.

His hand was on the receiver when he found himself looking into something small and blue and ugly, something he had seen once or twice before in his chequered career—the muzzle of a ·32 automatic. He didn't need to wait for the command. His hands shot up. His smile vanished and his good humour yielded to surly surprise.

" So that's how it is ! " he remarked.

" Mr Strong," the Ambassador told him, " you will please to remember that you are on Japanese soil while you are in this Embassy and that what I tell you to do, you must do. You may not telephone to anyone

nor may you leave the Embassy until I say. If you try to do either, you will be shot. Mr Tyler will show you where you are to stay."

Dennis and the burly newspaperman left the room together. As soon as they were in the hall, Strong dropped his hands and his subdued manner at the same moment. "Say, Tyler," he cajoled, "slip me the word, will you? What's all the shooting for? And why's everybody sitting round looking like scarecrows? This is big medicine, boy. Wild horses couldn't drag me out of this dump now."

"We'll see what White Horse can do," Dennis informed him. "Joe O'Connor's stuff is guaranteed free of fusil-oil, methyl—or is it ethyl?—alcohol, and his labels are unequalled out of Scotland. Come on down and Murray and I will tell you how the land lies."

A few moments later the three men were in the cool of the basement awaiting the arrival of the bootlegger.

"Bob," said Dennis, "Bill Strong wants to know what the trouble is about. He knows that Prince Hojo is here and when he tried to telephone the Ambassador pulled a gun on him. He'll play fair. Shall I tell him?"

"Certainly not!"

"Very well," Tyler continued. "Here's the story,

Bill. Hojo is in town, as you gathered from the Press release you saw in Urquhart's office—where *is* Frank, by the way——? "

" Haven't seen him all morning," the Englishman observed.

" Really? He's probably occupied in writing the biggest Press release of all time upstairs. To continue, Bill. Prince Hojo is in town but he's not to be seen. In fact, we don't know where he is, and as we don't want his presence known until it can be explained, we've been sitting up all night waiting for him. That's etiquette. Damned silly rot, no doubt, but that's the way things are done with Princes incog. My own guess is that he put up at some small hotel here and will be around later in the day."

" Say," Strong's voice was derisive, " do you expect me to swallow that? "

" Why not? " asked Tyler coldly. " You've swallowed nearly everything else available. You'll have to hold on to that just now—anyhow, here's Joe O'Connor."

A short stocky individual, with a pock-marked red face, a candid grey eye and a neat self-contained manner, appeared in the doorway, clad in spotless whites and chewing reflectively on a match. " Got

the hooch in the hall," he remarked. "The Jap's bringing it down."

Kanehira staggered into the kitchen carrying a case crammed with straw-clad bottles. Tyler rose and inspected it carefully. He studied the lettering on the box, removed the straw jacket from a bottle, and examined the label and the seal.

"It's a work of art, Joe," he said at last. "Even the revenue stamp is perfect. How *do* you do it?"

"Honest to God, Mr Tyler," O'Connor assured him professionally, "that stuff is straight off the boat."

"Oh, forget it!" interjected Strong. "Try a glass of this stuff and taste good whisky for once in your life."

O'Connor picked up the bottle of pre-War whisky, poured the remainder into a glass, and rolled it reflectively round his mouth. "Yeah," he admitted, "that's pretty good, if I say so myself. I ought to know. I made it."

Kanehira swiftly removed the litter of straw and the case from the kitchen and arranged the bottles neatly on top of the frigidaire. He brought clean glasses and some fresh cubes of ice and withdrew unobtrusively. O'Connor watched him closely. After he had gone, the bootlegger turned to the others.

"Say," he inquired, "who's that guy? I seen him before somewhere?"

"You're a pretty good man then," Tyler laughed. "He just arrived in town yesterday."

"No? Honest? I sure have set eyes on him somewhere round here. That's funny, ain't it? He ain't one of the regular Embassy servants. But I know I've seen him around town."

"Oh, forget it!" Bill Strong commanded again. "Come on and open up a bottle of your poison."

Four drinks were poured, ice tinkled pleasantly in four glasses, and a small quantity of water was added. "Here's how!" said Bill Strong. He stopped. "Say," he said, "do you smell smoke? I do."

The four men paused. A thick black finger of smoke was thrusting itself under the door which communicated with the cellar. Tyler sprang to his feet and pulled the door open. A black cloud rushed forth into the room with the spring of an angry beast and a red glare behind it cracked and hissed evilly. The Embassy was on fire!

II

FIRE !

UNTIL you have been caught in a burning house, it is useless to imagine how you will behave at the cry of " Fire ! " You may think you will be calm and sensible and find that you have thrown the Sèvres china out the window, walked downstairs with the sofa-cushions, and knocked the legs off the grand piano. You may dread the very thought of fire and when it comes find yourself so calm and efficient that when the panic is over you are the hero of the occasion. You may find that the people whom you think will need to be rescued are leading you downstairs or you may discover yourself labouring to end the hysterics of a man of fifty, who is well known for his common sense and unexcitable temperament. Fire is the most dangerous drug in the modern pharmacopœia, humanity's most incalculable stimulant.

The three old men were sitting quietly in the reception room when Kanehira dashed screeching into the room, pointing behind him into the hall. Three tired pairs of eyes followed his gesture and saw the faint curl of smoke as a whiff of scorching varnish and

burning wood crept into the room. "Fire!" They leaped to their feet, as if galvanized. Acorn gave a wild glance at the smoke and dashed out into the garden, clutching a glass in one hand and an empty siphon in another. The Secretary of State stood stock-still, looking round severely in all directions. The Ambassador rushed into the hall and ran upstairs to the room where lay the body of Prince Hojo. A moment later the Secretary followed him and arrived just in time to prevent the trembling envoy from flinging the shutters open and dragging the stiff body to the window, preparatory to letting it down into the street. The Secretary grasped the Ambassador's arm.

"Never do that way," he panted. "Help you take it downstairs."

One took the head and one the feet of the tragic burden and, gasping beneath the weight, were preparing to carry it down the flight of stairs and out of the Embassy when a voice called up to them, "Fire's out!" Hurriedly, avoiding each other's eyes, they carried the stiff figure back to the little room whence they had taken it and replaced it reverently on the improvised bier between the windows. They looked at each other once, walked silently out of the room, and closed the door. Still silent, the Ambassador reached out and clasped the blue-veined

knobbly hand of the Secretary of State. They shook hands understandingly and walked downstairs.

Peggy was still moping in the small downstairs reception room when the " Fire ! " call rang out. She did not move for a full two minutes, excited beyond the capacity for thought or action. Trembling with a wild exultation she walked to the hall. Smoke, dense black smoke, was pouring up from the stairway that communicated with the basement. Wisps of hot whitish vapour were seeping up through the parquet floor. The guard at the door was standing, a drawn pistol in his hand, glaring wildly at the smoke, but obviously determined not to leave his post. As she stood watching, Urquhart came blundering through the door of the big reception room behind her, looked round, started for the front door, saw the guard, and then ran down the stairs through the smoke. The smoke lessened abruptly and finally ceased, to be succeeded by the unmistakable stench of wet charred wood. A moment later she heard Murray's voice calling " All out ! " and he came bounding up the cellar-stairs, wet and grimy, and smiling. " First score for us," he remarked casually, sitting down on the stairs and lighting a cigarette.

When Tyler had opened the cellar door and discovered the fire the deadly calm of action came over

him. It was not his first encounter with fire and he had the advantage of having a definite object in view. His orders rang out like pistol-shots.

"Murray, watch the valet! Here, you two, put out that fire! Use the siphons! Use anything! It's not bad. I'll get Urquhart."

Stung into action by the unexpected lash of authority in his voice, the reporter and the bootlegger hurled themselves into the fray with the happy abandon of those who are destroying other people's property in a worthy cause. Lord Robert dashed out into the corridor and began a hasty search from room to room. Just at the foot of the stairs, he saw, was one of those glass-faced fire alarms, painted red, with its little red metal hammer attached by a short brass chain, resting on two brackets beneath it. Acting on impulse he leaped for it and had seized the hammer, when he heard footsteps running across the floor above him, toward the stairs. Again, some unaccountable impulse restrained him. He replaced the hammer and swung out of sight in the angle of the stairwell. Down the stairs, two steps at a time, came Kanehira, his face convulsed with terror. In a flash he seized the hammer and was about to strike when Murray reached forward and caught his arm. The man's face was a

study. For a moment he glared at the young Englishman like a wild animal. Then he jerked loose, ran
along the corridor into the kitchen, and joined the fire-
fighters. Murray still waited. Urquhart came down
the stairs on the run, hesitated for a moment, noticed
the British Chargé, and ran on to the kitchen. Murray
followed him. In a moment they were all at work,
choking and gasping in the fumes in the cellar. The
fire proved to be slight. A large pile of old newspapers
had caught and the flames were licking at the woodwork of a partition. A few siphons had extinguished
the blaze, and the slower, more difficult task of putting
out the smouldering embers was occupying the volun-
teer fire-brigade. After a while Joe O'Connor had an
idea and shovelled the entire mass of charred papers
into the furnace. The air gradually cleared and the
five men looked at each other.

" Nice fire," said Strong. " How about a drink? "
The idea seemed to be popular. Murray left the
four in the kitchen sampling the liquid rewards of
heroism from one of Mr O'Connor's well-blended bottles
while he went upstairs to pass the word that the fire
was over. He discovered Peggy looking like an excited
angel, standing by the door of the reception room; he
sat down on the stairs and lit a cigarette, only to

curse beneath his breath as a moment later he had
to move to let the Ambassador and the Secretary
come down.

At the alarm Tyler, instead of going up the stairs,
had turned out to the left at the end of the basement
passage and had gone through a little disused door
which led into the garden by means of a sunken flight
of stone steps. He was by no means certain what was
in his mind, but he felt an imperative necessity to
catch a glimpse of the entire theatre of operations
before making his next move. As he entered the garden
he saw that it had suddenly become popular. One of
the guards, who had been posted there the night
before, had emerged from his inconspicuous post
behind the arbour and was standing with drawn
pistol and an expression of benevolent curiosity upon
his face. " He'd shoot somebody for two cents! " was
Tyler's reflection as he passed. Acorn, holding his
glass and siphon, was standing reflectively by the little
sunken pool in the middle of the garden, eyeing the
wall as though he expected to scale its fifteen feet of
smooth brickwork with a single run and jump. Francis
Urquhart, seemingly distracted, was dodging back and
forth in front of the French windows which led into
the big reception room. As Tyler appeared, Urquhart

seemed to have made up his mind. He turned and dashed into the reception room.

Tyler ran after him. He flung open the door to find Urquhart holding the telephone receiver and jiggling the hook up and down frantically. The young diplomat rushed across the floor and put his hand over the mouthpiece.

" What are you doing? " he demanded.

Urquhart eyed him wildly. " Fire! " he gasped. " Got to call the Fire Department! "

Tyler glared at him. " I'm in charge here," he snapped. " You go down to the cellar and fight the fire. I'll call the Department."

Urquhart hesitated. Tyler was trembling with excitement, his eyes were gleaming with a queer light which Urquhart had never noticed before in the dapper young diplomat. " All right," he consented and ran stumblingly out into the hall, paused for a moment, and plunged through the smoke down the stairs to the basement.

" Number please? " The tinny voice over the wire was sarcastic.

" Main 4510," Tyler breathed into the mouthpiece, watching the door nervously.

" State? Give me Nichols . . . Captain Nichols?

. . . Tyler speaking. Japanese Embassy. Hold up all telegrams from here. Post guards on outside and arrest anyone attempting to leave grounds until further orders. . . . Charge? . . . Hell, man, charge it to the Secretary of State!" and hung up.

No sooner had he replaced the receiver on the hook than he jumped away from it as though it were a deadly serpent, ran to the far end of the reception room with a curious weaving motion of the hips that had been exceedingly troublesome once upon a time to some gentlemen from Yale who thought they knew how to play football, turned, and was casually lighting a cigarette when the Ambassador and the Secretary of State returned and resumed their seats by the telephone.

Tyler stepped into the garden. "Fire's out!" he called to Acorn, who had by this time carefully deposited his glass and siphon on the stone rim of the fountain and was chewing ruminatively on an unlighted cigar. The Under-Secretary grunted non-committally, glared at his subordinate, and walked back into the house without a word.

No sooner was the coast clear than the Chief of the C.P.I. walked swiftly to the end of the garden which lay nearest to the house. It was as he expected.

Opening from the cellar was another door, similar to the one which he himself had used to get quickly into the garden. He slipped swiftly down the stone steps and tried the door. It was firmly locked. He looked round. On the pavement, in the ruck of mud and dead leaves which the rain had washed down, lay a half-burned match.

"That," he remarked to himself, "just about tears it."

Somebody was very anxious to attract publicity to the strange situation in the Embassy, of that there could be no doubt. Had that somebody set fire to the papers in the cellar, come out of the door, locked it behind him, and then waited for a chance to start a fire alarm? Tyler could see the situation in his mind's eye, clearly. Francis Urquhart had been missing all morning, at least nobody had seen him. He had the run of the Embassy basement and, despairing of quick publicity, had set fire to the papers, let himself out of the cellar door, waited until the coast was clear, and then tried to call the Fire Department.

Tyler mopped his brow as he thought of the narrow escape, the engines tearing up Sixteenth Street with bells clanging, the throbbing, panting apparatus parked in front of the Embassy, the crowd which appears

from nowhere to watch a fire—" Good Lord, it's the Embassy! "—police cordons, firemen tramping in the front door, running their ladders up the walls, crashing into upper windows and then—publicity! PUBLICITY! Urquhart was a publicity man. Only he knew what publicity there would be, when the discovery was made that the Secretary of State, the British Chargé, two high State Department officials, the Japanese Ambassador and the daughter of the Senator from Massachusetts, were locked in the burning Embassy with the corpse of Prince Hojo of Japan. The biggest newspaper story of all time.

But what did it mean? Why did Urquhart want publicity? Was he on a false trail, after all? Might not that match have been dropped by a cigarette-smoker in the garden? Might not the papers have caught fire from spontaneous combustion, from defective wiring, by sheer accident? Might not Kanehira, maddened by grief at the death of his master, have decided to send the Prince to some Shinto Valhalla in a funeral pyre worthy of a Prince? Or was that exclusively a Scandinavian custom? Could he even assume that Urquhart's attempt to telephone the Fire Department was deliberate? Tyler knew that people acted foolishly in a fire. He was not so suspicious as

to make the traditional diplomatic blunder of assuming that everything was done with a deliberate end in view.

"I say, Dennis!" His thoughts were interrupted by Lord Robert, no longer cool and immaculate. "Do you know that I stopped that little valet chap from starting an alarm?"

Tyler went solemnly up to the young Englishman and shook his hand earnestly. "That's the best news I've ever heard," he said.

"I thought so myself. Do I get a Carnegie medal or the Order of the Bath?"

"Here's the way I see it——" began Tyler and told him.

Murray whistled melodiously. "That's pretty average sinister," he observed. "I don't like it. However," he added, "I don't see that we're much forrader."

"Well," Tyler admitted, "we're not. But at least we know this, that the two unaccounted members both so forgot themselves in a moment of general panic that they each independently tried to start a fire alarm. I said if we waited long enough the opposition would show its hand. I nominate Messrs Urquhart and Kanehira for the Opposition."

" I second the motion," retorted the Englishman, in his best Parliamentary manner, " but of the two Urquhart was miles away at the time and Kanehira was in the basement. How does that help me? "

" Hanged if I know, but at least we know whom to watch. That's something, and we still have twelve hours."

"THE LOTUS OF MANCHURIA"

THE sun rode high in the heavens now, pouring down upon the city an avalanche of fire. Built in a swamp on a tract of land so useless that only a Government could afford to buy it, hemmed in from any mercy of the wind by a circle of sun-baked hills, with the very river a brazen mirror which flung back the heat, Washington seemed determined to justify its reputation of the most stupidly located of tropical cities.

The silence in the Embassy had become intolerable as the heat. Every one was dirty, tired and discouraged. The stench of sodden ashes made the basement, though cool, unpleasant. The heat was driving the musty woolly odour of upholstery through the living-rooms, and the upper stories had already become a furnace, in which the sickish odour of blood lurked. Tyler went upstairs for a moment. He opened the door of the room where the dead Prince lay, and shut it hastily. Through the dense heat crept the odour of corruption.

The Chief of the C.P.I. sat down on the stairs and mopped his brow. Things were cooking up with a

vengeance. Lock seven men, a girl, and a corpse in a building on a stifling August Sunday, deprive them of food, sleep, and the sense of security, add to that the atmosphere of crime and high politics, and you have a devil's broth that needs little stirring. The sands were running out now. The time left to clear Murray was brief. If nothing had been changed by midnight Tyler saw the end clearly. Either Murray would be given a pistol and allowed to kill himself, or he would be locked up as insane. In either case a crisis so serious as to threaten war would be precipitated.

On the one hand, death or disgrace for Murray, permanent enmity between the Orient and the Anglo-Saxon world, and all the sorrow and waste and folly of international friction and the purposeless tragedy of war. And he had heat, discomfort, and a few hours to discover the alternative. It was not as though he had help. Lord Robert, for all his cool-headedness and British buoyancy, could do little. He was the accused. Too much zeal in clearing himself would only drag him farther into the quicksand. Peggy Lawrence was well-meaning but devoid of practical intelligence. Life was still a game to her, like tennis, to be played with pleasant partners and followed by refreshments in the shade. The Secretary could do

nothing. Acorn was virtually useless. The Ambassador seemed convinced of Murray's guilt. No help
there. The bootlegger and the reporter must not be
told anything which could possibly be kept from them.
At the end, they must be given the official version
which it was Tyler's duty to concoct, and uncere-
moniously turned out of the Embassy.

The 'opposition' had vaguely defined itself as consisting of Kanehira, Prince Hojo's valet, and Frank
Urquhart, the Embassy's Press Adviser, more by process of elimination than by evidence. That there was
an opposition had been made evident by the fire. It
was little enough to go on, especially as both men
had cast-iron alibis so far as the crime was concerned.
The Japanese guards who had been summoned to
protect the building were ruled out from the start. It
was impossible; Murray *had* to face the music, innocent
or guilty.

On the other hand, Tyler had two strong cards which
nobody suspected. The first was the cordon of men
whom Captain Nichols of the Departmental Guard was
stationing round the Embassy to arrest any fugitive.
If the murderer attempted to break away Tyler
would win. The second was nerves—nerves worn
ragged by heat, hunger, alcohol, and fear. One break

E

had been made—the fire—but beyond advancing the atmosphere of crisis, it had not given a clue.

A clue—a clue—some weakness in the opposition, some line of attack. Some way to precipitate the action which would carry him on to the checkmate. The problem was as smooth and innocent as an egg. There was nothing to take hold of. Take Kanehira, for example, who had been Hojo's valet-guardian for twenty years, Kanehira, who had been in the United States only a few days and whose loyalty was as unquestioned as that of the Ambassador himself. But was it? Could one be sure that he had not been tampered with by some outside agency? What was that secret organization, anyhow? The Black Dragons. Could they be concerned in it?

A little question began tickling his mind. Joe O'Connor had seen Kanehira before, somewhere, somehow, he said. How could a Washington bootlegger have seen the valet of a Japanese Prince? Yet O'Connor had the hard, photographic memory for faces that is the underworld's great asset in the struggle for existence. Couldn't something be tried there?

Tyler sighed and walked downstairs to where Peggy was sitting, listlessly wondering what she could do.

" Peggy," he whispered.

She looked up and smiled, wanly.

" Peggy, you can help me."

" How ? " She was not over-eager.

" Wait till I have gone downstairs, then ring the bell for Kanehira. Ask him to bring you a weak whisky-and-soda. And look at him carefully. Tell me later whether you have ever seen him before."

Peggy cheered up. " A whisky-and-soda sounds wonderful," she admitted, " but of course I've seen him before. I saw him this morning and I saw him yesterday."

Dennis groaned, clutched his fiery red hair with both hands, and tore it symbolically.

"Oh, I see," Peggy announced brightly. "You mean, whether I saw him before I came to the Embassy ? "

" Go to the head of the class! Now, wait until I've been gone a few minutes and then ring for him. And try to look at him as though he weren't just somebody whose job it is to bring you drinks when you ring for them, but as though he were somebody you might have met at a dance. Do you understand ? "

The girl was all eagerness now. " Of course I do," she said. " Just like waiters and your partners wearing dress-suits. You see one and you don't see the other."

Tyler laughed. "You've got a wonderful brain, Peggy. It's a pity you don't go in for diplomacy."

He lounged casually away, down the smoke-grimed stairs, along the basement corridor and into the kitchen, where O'Connor, Murray and Bill Strong were drinking seriously and steadily, while the frigidaire worked furiously to make them more ice and Kanehira was busying himself rinsing glasses and emptying ash-trays. Tyler helped himself to a stiff drink, stirred it vigorously until the fizz had gone from the sodawater, and took a long, sweet pull. There was a short angry buzz on a bell and a little arrow jerked into a vertical position in the indicator over the door. Kanehira looked knowingly at it, pushed the plunger which put it back into place, and hurried noiselessly away, walking on the balls of his feet with the silent, level gait of the trained servant.

Tyler waited until he was out of the room and then turned to the others. "O'Connor," he said, "you say you think you've seen that valet before. Take a good look at him the next time he comes into the room and see if you can remember where you saw him. You too, Bill. You go everywhere and know everybody. I've got a hunch," he added, "that there's something queer about him."

The four men sat silently, waiting. The door opened

and Kanehira reappeared. He deftly arranged a tray with a tall glass and some cubes of ice and a small pony of whisky. In a moment he was gone.

"Well, Joe," asked Tyler, "what's the answer?"

O'Connor scratched his head. "It beats me," he admitted. "He somehow makes me think of a theatre. Like I told you. But I can't place him."

"How about you, Bill?" Tyler inquired. "Did you spot him?"

"Well-l," Strong drawled. "I can't say that I did. But somehow Hollywood and a wild party I once had there with O'Donoghue of the Paramount Press Bureau comes into my head."

Dennis laughed. "Hot stuff!" he commented. "The trouble with you both is the movies. He looks like the Japanese valet who is standard equipment with every Hollywood Society Drama, that's all."

"Nonsense!"

The three men turned curiously and faced Murray, with some surprise, for he had been doing his drinking silently.

"I tell you what you're all thinking of. He's a dead ringer for that Japanese actor chap who's been doing that series of films at Hollywood. What's his name? Hiki? That's it."

"Aw, nuts!" said Strong.

O'Connor said nothing. His bright eyes glanced from one to the other. *He* wasn't goin' to do no buttin' in on this game, whatever it was. The Englishman was right, all right, but *he* was goin' to keep his nose clean.

"If only," Tyler sighed petulantly, "all Japanese did not look so exactly like each other, it would be so much simpler."

He finished his drink quickly and walked upstairs. He passed Kanehira on the way and smiled at him pleasantly. Yes, there *was* something oddly familiar about him.

He found Peggy, her nose buried in a glass filled with a pale amber fluid in which swam square lumps of ice.

"This is wonderful," she exclaimed, "I promise never to feel sorry for Commander Byrd again."

"Well," Dennis demanded, "what about the valet?"

"Why, do you know, he is just like Hiki, who plays the hero in *The Lotus of Manchuria*."

"I see," said Tyler drily. "So you and Bob have been going to the movies?"

Peggy Lawrence blushed. "Who told you that?" she demanded.

Tyler looked mysterious. "We have—er—ways of our own," he admitted, "of—er—knowing these things."

" Well, at any rate, it's a glorious play, all about an American girl who becomes the adopted daughter of a mandarin. She is kidnapped by a horrible brigand who wants her to marry him, but she's in love with a young Japanese nobleman who's in exile because he had refused to marry the girl his father had chosen for him. He heard of her danger and rescued her and he and the villain have a wonderful fight all over the Great Wall of China and then he discovers that all the time she was the girl his family wanted him to marry. They have lots of fighting and warships and automobile wrecks and camels."

Tyler was horrified. " Child," he said severely, " your taste is utterly debased. I know exactly how it all happens and I bet that there are a couple of comedy American negroes who are members of the bandit army and that the bandits never ride anywhere without singing a deep rollicking bass chorus about ' A Life on the Rolling Yak ' or words to that effect."

" How did you know ? Oh, Dennis, you've seen it yourself and have been teasing me all along."

" I haven't seen it," fervently protested Dennis, " but I know Hollywood," he added darkly.

Leaving the girl, Tyler strolled into the next room, where, he noticed, the three old men had been joined by

Urquhart, who had taken advantage of the general pause to wash himself and make himself fairly presentable.

"Mr Ambassador," said Tyler, "are you entirely sure of the identity of Kanehira?"

The diplomat looked up in surprise. "Of course I am, Mr Tyler," he replied.

Urquhart's lip curled with amusement. "If you care to come to my office," he said, "I can show you Kanehira's biography in the confidential file, if the Ambassador permits. He's perfectly straight."

"Of course he's straight," Tyler agreed. "It's only that at least two people here have thought that he looks remarkably like the great Japanese cinema actor Hiki, and I wanted to make sure who he was."

"I can assure you that Kanehira is not a cinema actor and is perfectly well known to me," the Ambassador informed him. "Kanehira has only been in this country a few days and has spent all his life in the service of the Imperial Household."

Tyler thought that there was a note, just a note, of urgency in Urquhart's voice as he chimed in, "Why, the thing's ridiculous! Hiki has been in this country for years and besides he's out in Hollywood now working on a new film."

"How do you know?" Tyler inquired.

Urquhart smiled silkily. "Because I brought him to this country in the first place. You may remember," he continued, turning to the Secretary, "a couple of years ago when there was all that fuss about Hollywood putting Japanese villains in its films. At that time I got in touch with the Hays organization and got them to take on Hiki. It's all part of our general publicity programme for better relations between the two countries."

The Secretary nodded. "I remember," he agreed.

Tyler smiled. "Well, I guess it's just a false trail, but I could have sworn there was something in it."

Urquhart was insistent. "What could there have been in it, anyhow?" he asked. "It's absolutely impossible and even if it were possible how would it help Murray?"

"I'm beginning to think you're right," Tyler agreed. "Poor Murray! I don't see how he could have done it but I don't see how to prove he didn't, unless I could prove that Kanehira did."

"Kanehira is above suspicion," the Ambassador declared, severely and with absolute finality.

IV

THE BLACK DRAGONS

THE afternoon was wearing on. Nerves were getting tenser. The heat was as fierce as ever, although the sun was already slanting toward the west. The air was so still that the smoke of Tyler's cigarette made a straight line as it rose from the garden walk, where he had thrown it. He sighed. From his post of vantage he could watch the house. Beside him sat Lord Robert, his head in his hands, with unseeing eyes and a vacant expression on his face. Through the open windows leading to the reception room came a snarl and wrangle of voices as the Secretary and the Under-Secretary, in the savage weariness of utter boredom, were arguing about some minor point of international law. An occasional clink from the open basement window told that Kanehira was still attending to the monumental thirst of Bill Strong and Joe O'Connor. Tyler idly wondered why the bootlegger had not attempted to leave, entirely unaware that O'Connor had sized up the guard at the Embassy door the moment he had entered and, having had on several occasions in his life to shoot his way out of a

house, had decided that it was safer, as well as more interesting, to stick around for a while and see what happened. Of Peggy and the Ambassador there was no sign, and the rattle and chatter of a portable typewriter from Urquhart's basement office indicated the latter's whereabouts.

" All present or accounted for," murmured Dennis, rubbing his hand languidly, yet with a certain amount of masculine pride, against the reddish stubble of beard on his square-set chin. " Robert, my man, can you spare me a cigarette? "

" Eh? What's that? " Murray came out of his brown study with an apologetic jerk.

" A cigarette, Robert," demanded Dennis firmly, extending his hand.

" I haven't got one," the Chargé replied, " and what's more, there isn't one in the entire Embassy. I asked everybody, even the guards."

" Good God! " the Chief of the C.P.I. exclaimed with honest indignation, " do you mean to tell me that we come on a party like this without enough tobacco to enable me to think. Ah, well, these inscrutable Orientals! Now I'll have to ask the Ambassador for a cigar." He leaped to his feet with decision.

The Chargé d'Affaires smiled. " No cigars either,"

he said. " I gather that's what started your Secretary of State and the Under-Secretary arguing about the Law of Angary."

Dennis subsided. " My God! " he gasped, " No tobacco! Now we *shall* see action! How long has this been going on? "

" Oh, about ten minutes. Just wait and you'll hear about it."

He was right. In the course of a few minutes the Secretary, Acorn, Urquhart and Peggy all drifted casually out and inquired whether Tyler had any cigarettes. Kanehira popped up the sunken stairs to say that the gentlemen in the kitchen would be very much obliged, please, for some cigarette-smoke. There were fifteen minutes of searching and questioning, and then the horrible fact dawned that there was nothing more to smoke in the entire Embassy. Suddenly Tyler had a thought. In the room with the corpse he had noticed a packet of cigarettes lying on the window-sill where Murray and the Prince had left them during their fatal encounter of the day before. The Chief of the C.P.I. jumped to his feet and, without a word to his companion, hurried into the Embassy. He ran upstairs to the door which stood half-hanging, half-leaning in its shattered frame.

Tyler braced himself and entered the room quickly. The scent of corruption was heavier in the air and some flies were buzzing busily. . . . The room swam slightly before Tyler's eyes. Conquering a sickening surge that shook his gorge, he ran to the window. He was right. There on the ledge lay an open packet of cigarettes, half used. He grasped them, started to put them in his pocket, then stopped, flung open the shutter and threw the packet out of the window into the street. He closed the shutter and went back to the garden.

Murray eyed him with concern. " What's new ? "

" Nothing," Tyler told him. " I have just performed a deed for which I deserve to be put in the history books. I have thrown a packet of cigarettes out of the window."

" Crazy fool ! " Murray muttered savagely. " I would give my life for an honest gasper."

" That's just it ! Perhaps you've never thought how dependent we all are on tobacco. The old and honourable Secretary may have physical and mental hardening of the arteries and all that, but he smokes six Havana cigars every day of his life. Old Acorn smokes a pipe for preference and stinks up the whole third floor of the Department with it. You, Peggy, I,

all get through the best part of a packet of cigarettes on ordinary days. Bill Strong smokes anything and at any time. Joe O'Connor chews and he came out without his plug. I've hardly ever seen Frank Urquhart without a cigarette in his hands and most of these Japanese servants use snuff. People can stand heat and hunger, but if you cut off their tobacco you'll have a revolution on your hands. That's what's happened now. I give them another hour to start something. And I'm not certain but that I'll start it myself."

Lord Robert sighed. " Wake up, old man," he said despondently. " It's all a dream. The only thing I'm certain of is a table, pen and ink, and a loaded pistol at midnight. I wish to God, Dennis, you'd do *something*. You have all these ideas but nothing happens. Peggy is one of God's sweetest fools but even she is working harder than you are. Why, she told me that she was going to have a long talk with the Ambassador this afternoon and tell him I was innocent. Fat lot of good it will do, but after all—well, you act as though it were a game and a chance to be clever—and I——" he broke off, eloquently.

" Cheer up! " Dennis advised with gruff intensity. " Don't think that just because I act like a silly ass I

am one. That's the mistake most Americans make about you English, but it's the first time I've seen you taken in by it. Just trust good old Tyler and the C.P.I. to pull you through. And just remember that I *must* treat it as a game and *must* be clever at it. If I take it seriously, I'll be sure to bungle it. Trust good old Dennis and I swear you won't take the leading *rôle* in your own funeral."

" But——" began Murray.

" Shush!" exclaimed Dennis, with exaggerated loudness, " here's Peggy. Well, Miss Lawrence, and how did your talk with his Excellency come off? "

" He was perfectly horrid," she exclaimed. " He wouldn't say a thing about Robert. Not a thing! I asked him all sorts of questions and he answered them perfectly nicely but when I asked him to believe a— a woman's heart and let Robert go, he simply turned away."

" Bless you, Peggy," said Murray fondly. " You mustn't go round worrying about me. I'll pull out of this all right. The Ambassador has had a hard knock, so you mustn't be too hard on him. After all, it does look as though I were guilty, but Dennis here is going to fix things up for me, somehow."

" Oh, how? " she demanded.

Tyler smiled wrily. " Somehow," he said. " Suppose you tell me what you and the Ambassador talked about."

" Oh, principally about Japanese politics. I asked him whether there weren't any Japanese organizations which would be glad to kill the Prince. He looked very angry and said no Japanese would think of such a thing. Then I said, ' Why not ? ' and he said a lot of things about shinto and bush—bush——"

" Bushido ? " Tyler suggested.

" Yes, that was it, and the samurai. Then I asked him whether there were any secret societies in Japan, like the Black Hand or the Ku Klux Klan. And he said that there was one patriotic society called the Black Dragons, but that it wasn't really secret and that everybody knew about it. So I asked him what the Black Dragons wanted and he said that they wanted Japan to make an alliance with Russia and China against the rest of the world, but nobody ever paid any attention to them and that the police could stop them any minute they made trouble. I asked if the Black Dragons ever killed anybody and he said that they had killed a few coolies to protest against the American Immigration Law and the Singapore Naval Base. I said that seemed a funny way of

protesting and why didn't they kill Americans or British people if they wanted to protest and he said that the police in Japan watched the foreigners to keep them from that sort of danger. Once, he said, some patriotic Japanese a long time ago had killed some British people and it had cost them too much."

Tyler whistled, " That must have been the Richardson murder," he commented. " You know, Robert, the time they knocked 'em on the Yedo road."

"Yes," Murray answered. "I've been thinking of that business ever since this began. We sent our fleet out there and bombarded them. Handy little precedent, eh?"

" Then I asked the Ambassador," Peggy continued valiantly, " whether the Black Dragons ever did anything outside of Japan. He said not much, not even in Manchuria, though he did admit that they had done some things in China. 'Such as?' I asked and he said 'Oh, nothing much.'"

" The reason being, my dear girl," Tyler drawled, " that he could hardly tell you that the Black Dragons had dynamited the governor of the most prosperous Chinese province and had installed a chap of their own choice. It took a British gunboat twenty minutes and the Foreign Office three years to straighten out that little show. But continue—pray continue——"

"Oh, there's nothing much more to say. I asked him if there were any Black Dragons—it's all terribly like Mah-Jong, you know, Flowers and Winds and Dragons—in America, and he said he believed not. I asked him if the murder of the Prince wouldn't help the Dragons and he said perhaps it would, but they had nothing to do with it as they would never kill a Prince of the Imperial Family. Then I told him Robert hadn't ever done it and he didn't say anything."

Murray smiled affectionately. "Thanks no end, Peggy," he said. "I'm afraid it's no go, but you did your best, anyhow."

"It's nothing," Peggy said gruffly. "Nothing!" she added softly.

Tyler stood up and gazed down at her judicially. "My dear," he observed, "with a head like yours you've simply got to marry a diplomat. Excuse me, will you, I want to think!"

The Black Dragons again. *Could* they have anything to do with this crime? He tried to remember what he had learned about them in Tokio. A super-patriotic group who hated the West and wanted Japan to lead in Asia. Patriotism was an intoxicant in most countries. In Japan it was a religion. Even the Black

Dragon passwords showed that : the two Elder Statesmen : " Togo "—the hero of the Russo-Japanese War
—and " Goto "—the great Prime Minister and diplomat. " Togo ! " and " Goto ! " " Togo ! " the password, and " Goto ! " the countersign. He'd always
wanted to try " Togo " on a Black Dragon but he'd
never had a chance. What a pity Kanehira was above
suspicion and the Black Dragons too hopelessly
patriotic to be involved.

The stubborn little facts, however, simply refused
to settle themselves symmetrically in his mind. It
was an attractive hypothesis, no doubt, to assume that
it was a political murder, engineered by the Black
Dragon Society for the purpose of getting rid of a
Prince who openly stood for Japanese co-operation
with the Anglo-Saxon Powers, and at the same time
causing a big international row which would fling
Japan headlong into the Asia for the Asiatics move-
ment. But it didn't hold water. It was on a par with
the silly story that the Austro-Hungarian General Staff
had planned the Sarajevo murders because they dis-
liked Franz Ferdinand's policy toward the Slavs. Of
course, the possibility that the murder had been an
accident remained. As Peggy had pointed out, Murray
and Prince Hojo had been dressed enough alike to

have been confused in the semi-darkness of a shuttered room, if the murderer were in a hurry, as he probably had been. It was an attractive theory, but it had to be laid aside again, simply because it had no relation to the facts.

"Facts are stubborn things," Dennis reflected, with marked unoriginality. "Of the only two people who might have committed it, one was miles away and the other is above suspicion."

"I wish to God," he continued, "that there wasn't so much brain-work to diplomatic detection. When the police have a case to solve all they have to do is to draw lots as to whom they shall arrest and then hit him with a rubber hose until he signs a confession. Then he is tried and acquitted because he is good to his mother or is a member of the Elks and the case is closed. Even in the Howard murder I had dear old Clovis Brown to worry and poor old woolly Pelton to suspect. But here I either have to admit that Murray did it or try to prove to old Kondo that it was just the fairies."

He paused and looked round him. Peggy and Robert were sitting close together in the arbour, talking with animation. Urquhart suddenly appeared at one of the French windows. He beckoned to Tyler. The Chief of the C.P.I. sauntered over.

" Got a cigarette, Frank? " he inquired.

" I wish to God I had," Urquhart remarked bitterly. His face was drawn and his fingers were twitching slightly.

" What's the trouble? " Tyler continued. " You look as though you have bad news."

" I have," Urquhart said, " I have something very serious to tell you."

" Great grief! " Tyler answered airily. " Has Mr Acorn persuaded the Secretary of State that international law is worth the paper it's written on or has the bootlegger bitten the Ambassador? "

" The Ambassador is going to telegraph Tokio."

V

THE TELEGRAM TO TOKIO

"SO he wants to send a telegram to Tokio, does he?" inquired Tyler. "Dear, dear me. How utterly and incomprehensibly diplomatic! If a diplomat wants to blow his nose, part his hair, or change over to a new brand of bird-seed for the canary, my dear Frank, does he go ahead and do it? No, decidedly not. He spends a great deal of perfectly valuable money wrung from the never-too-enthusiastic taxpayer to send a telegram requesting instructions. At least that's the case with us, although I always understood that the Imp. Jap. Govt. was above such foolery."

Behind the mask of trivial banter Tyler had come to life. His blue eyes were sparkling and his unregenerate red hair was gloriously confused. What had once been a very good morning suit before it had been smeared with ashes, slept in, and lived in for twenty-four sweltering hours, combined with his unshaven visage, made him look like an unusual type of tramp.

The period of waiting was at an end. Something in his bones told him that the period of action, the mad fifteen minutes for which he had been working, was

in sight. What had been a crazy problem in human statics had subtly changed into a new and dynamic form. Urquhart seemed terribly agitated. He was quivering with nervousness; the perspiration was streaming down his face, although the sun had set and the air was cooling rapidly.

" Don't joke," the Press Adviser begged, " this is damned serious. Something's got to be done. The Ambassador says he's got to telegraph Tokio. It's standing instructions in his service. An Ambassador is allowed to handle a case on his own initiative but must report to Tokio within twenty-four hours, no matter how he has handled it."

" What an intelligent way to do things," commented the Chief of the C.P.I., " though the good Lord knows that if some of our Ambassadors were allowed to use their own judgment they would bring on a world war in half a day. It's funny that his Ex. didn't say anything to me about it. He gave me his word I should have till midnight and we still have five hours at least to go."

" Somebody's *got* to stop him," said Urquhart vehemently. " We can't have that story getting out over there now."

" What does the Ambassador intend to say, Frank ? "

" He says he will tell the Foreign Office in absolute confidence that the Prince has met with a serious accident and that he will wire full details to-morrow, but he feels he should give them some warning."

Tyler nodded. " That makes sense to me," he agreed, " let him go ahead and send it."

Urquhart turned on him, his eyes blazing, his fists clenched tight, his voice hoarse with suppressed excitement. " I tell you, Tyler," he exclaimed, " he mustn't be allowed to send it. You don't know Tokio as I do. Once a telegram like that gets in the F.O., everybody knows it. Why——"

" They don't seem to have any difficulty keeping some things quiet," Tyler observed, " if they really want to."

" But don't you see, in this case, they won't want to ? They won't see the reason for keeping it quiet. They'll want to prepare public opinion and let it out gradually. Tyler, you've *got* to persuade Viscount Kondo not to send that telegram."

Tyler laughed. " Hoity-toity, good old Frank, but you *are* in a taking. The only man who has the right to say ' got ' to me is that venerable thunderbolt who goes by the title of the Secretary of State, and *he* has too much sense. However, I'll see his Excellency and try to discover why all this mad rush."

To tell the truth, Tyler was completely nonplussed. His theory—suspicion was too strong a word—that Frank Urquhart might in some way be involved in the crime, rested solely on the assumption that the Press Adviser wanted to produce publicity as soon as possible. This assumption, in turn, rested on the general idea that the function of a publicity man is to procure publicity and on the specific fact that Urquhart had tried to call the Fire Department during the excitement of the fire. Flimsy enough evidence it was, gossamer-thin stuff from which to weave the garb of innocence for Robert Murray, but it was all he had. And now Urquhart was begging him to help keep the crime secret.

He found the Ambassador seated alone by the telephone. The Secretary and Acorn had disappeared, and Tyler suspected that they had gone to the cellar to have a drink—a surmise in which he was, unfortunately, entirely correct.

" I beg your pardon, your Excellency," he inquired suavely, " is it correct that you are going to cable Tokio now instead of waiting until midnight? "

Kondo nodded his head slowly, his eyes fixed inscrutably on Tyler.

" Do you think it will be altogether safe? " Tyler

inquired. " Will there be no danger of publicity at the other end? "

" There should be none, Mr Tyler," the old diplomat assured him. " I plan to send it in our most confidential code and only say enough to prepare the Foreign Minister for the terrible shock he will receive later."

" But, Mr Ambassador," Tyler pleaded, " you yourself assured me that you would do nothing until midnight to-night and I have been working on that assumption. We don't dare risk the slightest leak now."

Kondo raised his hand, the gnarled, yellow claw of an old man. " I am sorry," he said. " When I gave you that assurance I entirely forgot my instructions that in any matter of importance I must—*must*," he repeated—" inform my Government within twenty-four hours. When I accepted this mission, I swore to abide by my instructions at all costs. My word to my Emperor must outweigh my word to you. I am sorry. I promised you without thinking. I am very sorry."

Tyler reflected. He knew the unwritten code of honour which ran through all diplomatic services and which was stronger even than instructions. He smiled.

" There is no need to be sorry, your Excellency," he said. " Your promise to me is of no importance. I

shall of course stand aside. After all, if the telegram goes in your secret code there will be little danger of its leaking out in Tokio."

"Absolutely none," the Ambassador assured him. "No one but the Foreign Secretary and his *Chef du Cabinet* have access to the code which I am going to use."

Urquhart started forward from beside Tyler, where he had been standing, listening in silence to the interchange. He seemed almost beside himself with anxiety.

"Your Excellency," he objected hoarsely, "do you consider it wise to use the secret code? It might happen that the Foreign Secretary and his assistant would be out of Tokio for the day. If I may make a suggestion, I would say send the telegram in one of the ordinary codes, marked 'Confidential,' and then it will be sure to be received. You could word it so that no undue alarm would be taken and it would take much less time than the triple code you use for highly confidential purposes."

The Ambassador looked gravely at Tyler. "What do you think of that, Mr Tyler?"

Tyler's brain was in a whirl. A few minutes ago Urquhart had been begging him to prevent the dispatch of the telegram. Now he was proposing that it be sent in a common code, one which might be read

by fifty people in the Foreign Office and be in every Tokio newspaper by Monday morning. He was about to dissent vigorously when a little inner voice began whispering to him, "*Ride it, you fool, ride it! Here's the break!*" The tingling pervasive sense of something about to happen fluttered like wings through the darkening Embassy. Something was about to happen! Something was about to happen! That intuition which is the better part of genius gathered from every corner of the room, swam like a fiery invisible cloud between him and the others. The moment etched itself deep into his consciousness like a room seen in a flash of lightning.

"A good idea," Tyler drawled, hardly able to keep his voice steady. "It will have to be cleverly worded, to avoid arousing suspicion. I think, your Excellency, that Mr Urquhart knows your way of doing things better than I do. May I suggest that you authorize him to prepare a draft of a telegram at once for your approval and then, if it is satisfactory, he could encode it and send it at once?"

The Ambassador reflected. "I agree, Mr Tyler. Urquhart, will you prepare the telegram?"

The Press Secretary fairly shot out of the room, energy and elation in his stride. The moment he was gone, Tyler turned abruptly to the Ambassador.

" Mr Ambassador," he said tensely, " where do you keep the secret code ? "

The Ambassador hesitated.

" Don't think I want to know for any silly purpose, sir," Tyler begged him. " It is terribly important to know where the code is now."

Viscount Kondo smiled. Everything was going to pieces now. Nothing mattered much longer. In a few minutes news of his disgrace would be on the way to Tokio and he would be ready to bring a long and honourable career to a close.

" The secret code," he said tonelessly, " is kept in the green safe in the little upstairs anteroom."

" Is that where you keep the code which will be used for the telegram Mr Urquhart is preparing ? " continued Tyler.

" Oh, no," the Ambassador said. " The ordinary codes are kept in the safe in the Chancery. Mr Urquhart has a duplicate set in his office for special or urgent work."

A flash of blinding comprehension came to Tyler. The luck had turned. " Will you let me see the inside of the safe upstairs, Mr Ambassador ? " he begged.

The Ambassador shook his head, decisively. " That," he said, " is contrary to my instructions."

The blood was dancing in Tyler's veins. "Quite so!" he agreed. "Then I beg you, Mr Ambassador, under no circumstances to leave the telephone during the next hour. There is terrible danger near at hand, and you must not let yourself be lured away."

The old man's expressionless eyes fixed themselves upon the Chief of the C.P.I. "I see," said Viscount Kondo. "I will not leave the telephone, Mr Tyler, until midnight."

"Thank you, sir," Tyler fervently assured him. "And please, sir, not a word of this to any of the others."

He was just in time. Frank Urquhart reappeared, with a sheet of typewritten paper. "Here's the telegram," he said.

"Read it!" the Ambassador ordered.

Urquhart began. "Most Confidential. His Imperial Highness Prince Hojo has met with a serious accident under circumstances threatening difficulties with other naval Powers. Little hope entertained for his recovery——"

"That," Tyler reflected, "is most assuredly true. Truth is a pearl more worn in the breach than the observance in diplomacy."

"And"—Urquhart's voice droned on—"I feel it my duty to inform your Excellency that the most

serious consequences are likely to follow. I am consulting informally with my British colleague and with the Secretary of State and will report full details to-morrow. I respectfully suggest news be regarded as highly confidential and communicated only to Imperial Family, Admiralty, General Staff, and Prime Minister with customary non-communicative warnings to Embassies at London, Paris, Rome, Moscow, and Legation at Peiping. Suggest usual preliminary naval dispositions and suspension of gold payments by Imperial Bank of Japan. (Signed) Kondo."

" That," said Tyler, still to himself, " is about as gentle a way of breaking it as turning in a fire alarm. If that doesn't start Tokio buzzing I'm a Dutchman."

Aloud he remarked, " That's a very good telegram, your Excellency. I suggest that Mr Urquhart encode it immediately."

The Ambassador nodded again and turned away.

" How long will it take, Frank? " Tyler asked.

" Oh, not more than half an hour at the outside! "

" I tell you what," suggested the Chief of the C.P.I., " let's both have a good stiff drink right away."

" I'll join you later," Urquhart informed him. " I'd better get this done first."

" Speak for yourself. Though I must say you have

a positively Quixotic attitude towards duty. Thank God I never learned how to send a code in my life. It's a dirty job and, once you know how, everybody makes you do it. And most of the things that are coded don't matter, anyhow."

" This does," Urquhart reminded him suavely.

" You're absolutely right, it does," said Tyler, " but now the die is cast and we're going to see a little fun, aren't we? "

VI

A GAME OF POKER

JAMES B. ACORN was puzzling his head to determine what all this reminded him of. That time he was defending the Japanese kidnappers before a San Francisco jury? Or the time in San Joaquin when he was prosecuting attorney and the friends of the accused tried to shoot it out during the noon recess?

Then a little picture formed in his head, a hot Tennessee sun, a sweltering court-room, a young school-teacher on trial for Baptist heresy, Clarence Darrow joshing William Jennings Bryan, and the newspaper boys drinking mountain whisky behind the court-house. Acorn had been retained as counsel, but had looked the case over and decided to stand clear of it; he would need the Southern California Methodist vote in his next campaign. But he had hung around Dayton for a few days and seen the modern inquisition at work and had wondered a little.

The recollection made him thirsty. It also reminded him of poker, of those all-night jack-pots with the prosecution and the newspaper boys, and the mellow

corn whisky which seemed to circulate so freely and naturally in the homely little gatherings. He finished his drink abruptly, turned to the Secretary with a sheepish grin, and nodded toward the kitchen—they were drinking in the decent retirement of Urquhart's office while the latter was thumbing codes and scrawling gibberish on a sheet of foolscap.

" Guess I'll start a little game," he said.

The Secretary eyed him coldly. " God help them! " was his unkind comment. " I know nothing about it. If you want me, you'll find me upstairs with the Ambassador. That damned fool, Tyler, is with him now and I don't trust that boy alone. He's made more trouble for me," he added bitterly, " than any two foreign Governments."

Acorn chuckled. " Why don't you send him to Siam? " he inquired.

" For the simple reason," snapped the old man, " that I don't want to wake up some morning and read that Siam has voted to be annexed to the United States. The only place I trust Tyler is where I can see him. Otherwise, I would have kicked him out of the service years ago. Don't win too much of their money, Acorn," he added. " Just remember that those boys haven't got the Power Trust behind them."

" Trust me ! " Acorn agreed. " I won't win a cent more than they have."

Fifteen minutes later, Mr Acorn was not so certain about his opponents having no Big Business connexions. Three-handed poker is a cut-throat game at best and even the former attorney for the utility interests can lose a lot of money at table-stakes when he is being scientifically whipsawed by the shrewdest poker-player in the Gridiron Club and by a wet-goods artist who has dropped fifty thousand at the races in a single afternoon without the flicker of an eye. Acorn began to play his cards close to his chest and to study his opponents. Bill Strong played a jovial impenetrable game in which a pair of threes, a bust, or a full house were equally undiscernible until the hands were shown. The bootlegger was calm and cold and his voice displayed no interest one way or another; win or lose, O'Connor had a roll of twenty grand he was prepared to risk. When he lost that there were a hundred thousand more in a Baltimore bank he could draw on. But he didn't expect to draw on it. Bill Strong entered the game with a hundred dollars in cash, a thousand dollars in the bank, and the comforting assurance that he had never yet risen from a poker game the poorer.

After his fifth big hand had been passed without an opposing bet and after he had lost three hundred dollars on small hands, Acorn began to think that straight poker was a bit too much of a gambling game for a married man.

"Boy," he boomed to Kanehira, "bring us all something more to drink. What's that? No more ice! Well, *make* some more ice! And say"—he turned to the others—" let's go into Urquhart's room. It's cooler there and there's a better light. And how about changing this to jack-pot?"

Peggy and Robert were in the garden, where Tyler had left them. The surge of expectancy which had overwhelmed the Chief of the C.P.I. had not affected the garden. The young couple moved alone in a quiet world of their own, full of dark shadows and blazing raptures, beneath a mantle of unspoken sympathy and friendly silences.

Peggy was the first to speak. "I wish, Robert," she said, "there was something I could do. It's awful just waiting."

"My dear girl," he said, rousing himself, "nobody can do anything but wait. Tyler's idea is that perhaps somebody will get tired of waiting and give himself away."

" I know," the girl exclaimed vehemently, " but Dennis is a perfect pig. All he's thinking about is how to be clever and get promotion out of this."

Murray protested. " I say, that's rather strong. Dennis has never let anybody down that I know of."

" You don't know him," Peggy objected. " He was perfectly horrid to Cynthia that time her father was killed."

" After all," he objected, " he did marry the girl, so perhaps he wasn't so horrid as he seemed."

Peggy blazed out. " But why doesn't he *do* something? We haven't got much time left, and oh—Bob —nothing must happen to you."

Murray turned earnestly toward the girl. " Does it matter as much as that? " he asked.

" Of course it matters," she murmured. " You know it matters. Oh, Robert, promise me that nothing will happen to you! "

For answer, the young Englishman leaned toward her in the dusk and kissed her. " Nothing's going to happen," he assured her, " as long as you love me."

" But," she protested, " is there nothing I can do? "

The British Chargé reflected swiftly on the ancient Chinese proverb that the advice of a well-meaning woman can overthrow seven cities. Yet he was not

in a position to reject help of any sort, even though it might be embarrassing.

"Tell you what, Peg," he said. "Dennis has an idea that Kanehira knows something about all this. Suppose you keep your eye on him. He's probably downstairs looking after the merchants in the cellar. You could go down and say you were looking for the Secretary. I'll walk in with you——"

"Psst!" A short, cautious whistle interrupted his advice.

"What was that?" the girl demanded.

"Psst!" The sound was repeated.

"It's Dennis!" Murray exclaimed, pointing upward.

Framed in the window of an upper room at the end of the wing was the face of the Chief of the C.P.I. He was beckoning to Murray and a finger hastily laid on his lips enjoined silence. A gesture in the direction of Peggy and a violent shaking of the head indicated that Tyler wanted to see Robert alone.

"Psst!" This time it was Murray who whistled, warningly. Tyler's head jerked out of sight, only just in time to avoid detection, for Frank Urquhart appeared in the open French window of the reception room and glanced inquiringly around.

"Well," asked Murray, casually, "what's the trouble?"

Urquhart smiled slyly. "I thought I'd better tell you," he announced, "that the Ambassador's telegraphing Tokio. He's 'phoning in the code message now."

Murray whistled again. "That sounds sinister," he remarked. "What's the telegram?"

Urquhart smiled. "Sorry I can't tell you," he answered.

"I can guess," the Chargé observed ruefully. "Well, it's all over now, I expect."

Urquhart nodded. "Where's Tyler?" he inquired. "I promised I'd have a drink with him as soon as I got this off my chest."

"He may be down in the basement," Lord Robert suggested, with perfectly truthful mendacity. "Peggy and I were going down. I'll tell him you're looking for him, shall I?"

"Please do!"

No sooner were Peggy and Robert safely out of sight in the basement than Urquhart threw aside his mask of caution. He began pacing up and down rapidly. He wished that Tyler would hurry and join him. He would like to have Tyler where he could

watch him. He thought of that body upstairs and shuddered. He hoped, he didn't even dare admit to himself what he hoped. It was such an unexpected situation. If only the valet—— Where in hell was Tyler? Tyler wasn't a fool. But just the same Urquhart wondered whether he could unravel the mystery in time. Hell, time didn't matter. The news would be in Tokio in a few minutes and if he knew Tokio the news would be all over the Empire by morning. He shrugged his shoulders angrily. All that talk about Hiki. Such rot! As though he could be involved in this. The Black Dragons? Would anyone ever believe that the Black Dragons could ever have done such a stupid thing? However, it was all turning out for the best. What did it matter, now? Where in *hell* was Tyler? That whistling now, in the garden. He could have sworn there were different people whistling. Perhaps. Was Tyler upstairs after all? Well, it would be pleasant to have a drink now that it was almost over. By midnight it would be all settled. He paused irresolutely. Through the open windows came the drone of the Ambassador endeavouring to read off a code telegram.

" Here! " he heard the voice of the Secretary of State. " Perhaps I'll have better luck. Will you let

me try it? All right, young lady—N as in Nellie,
P as in 'Possum, O as in Oil, S as in Swanson, B as in
Borah, A as in Andrew. One word. C as in Coolidge,
U as in Utah——"

Urquhart frowned. At that rate it would be half
an hour before the message had been verified and put
on the wire. Should he go in and offer to help or
should he find Tyler? He paused irresolutely and then
entered the house. . . .

"Well, boys," Acorn beamed expansively. "This
is better!" He, Strong, and O'Connor were playing
pat hands with a stripped deck and he had won back
some of his money. The whisky he had consumed was
lending a mellow glow to his outlook on life, awakening
a strong poetic streak in him. He was in a mood to
weep at one of James Whitcomb Riley's poems or to
pick a fight with his best friend. Only he didn't have
a best friend. He had been in politics too long.

The three faces bent close over the table and watched
the fall of the cards, with the masked intensity of
expert gamblers. As they watched, a little blue light
flashed on over Urquhart's desk in the corner. It
was an inconspicuous light and would have conveyed
nothing to any of the players, even if they had noticed
it. It burned steadily for a few seconds and then

flashed off as abruptly as it had come on. Kanehira saw it, his brows puckered with surprise. He watched it come and go, then left the room in haste. None of the card-players noticed that he had gone and the game went on.

" Say," Acorn suggested, " this is the Japanese Embassy and I say we ought to play Japanese poker. We oughtn't to bet dollars. It's not respectful. We ought to bet yen."

" Yen," Strong repeated. " The only yen I ever had was one for a girl in a tea-house. I was stung at that," he added, immodestly. " The natives give 'em oranges."

" How about a drink? " O'Connor inquired. " This is on me."

" Kanehira! " Acorn's voice supplemented Strong's invocation with the famous call of the East: " Boy! "

There was no answer. " That's funny " said Strong, " he was here a minute ago."

O'Connor nodded. " The Jap left just about the time you was talking about yen."

" That's all right," Strong said. " He's gone upstairs, I guess. If he doesn't come back in a couple of minutes I'll get the drinks myself. Let's see now. What have we here? Ah, yes, the old familiar faces,

three of a kind and a little pair and it will cost you several yen to learn different. Five yen! "

" See you! " O'Connor observed. This was kind o' loony, he felt. The back of his head was beginning to prickle. There was shooting in the air, all right. He unobtrusively patted the pistol in his hip-pocket. Well, if they were shooting he was O.K. . . .

Kanehira felt trouble coming. Big trouble. He hurried away on noiseless feet, up the stairs and toward the second story. He did not notice a slight, white-clad figure which watched him. He had just started to mount the stairs which led to the upper part of the Embassy when he heard his name called. It was Miss Lawrence. She was panting slightly.

" Oh, Kanehira! " she said, " where have you been? The Ambassador has been calling for you, I think."

The valet stopped. His face was bland and impenetrable beneath the soft glow of the electric lights. He bowed and walked to the reception room, awaiting orders. Peggy waited until he had closed the door behind him. A moment later, she was racing up the stairs, three steps at a time.

DIPLOMATIC BURGLARY

DENNIS TYLER had strolled unobtrusively into the hall of the Embassy. Urquhart was down below at work on his coding. It would take him at least half an hour. That was short enough, but it would give Tyler time to examine the safe. The Chief of the C.P.I. had ridden his hunches before, and this was a strong one. For some reason or other, he felt, he must open that safe in the little upstairs anteroom. It held, somehow, the key to the whole mystery.

He was about to run upstairs, when his heart sank. The Secretary of State had appeared from the basement and was glaring at him balefully.

" Well, young man, " the old man snapped, " this is a fine to-do ! What's your plan now, hey ? "

" My dear Mr Secretary," Tyler assured him deferentially, " really in weather like this—— Well, sir, quite frankly, I don't think I'd better tell you my plans. You would very properly object to them. What you don't know can't hurt you and I'll resign to-morrow if you like."

" Resign ! " The Secretary was indignant. " Do

you think I'd ever let you resign? No, sir, you'll stay right here until I'm through with you. And when I *am* through with you, I hope to have the pleasure of firing you! What's your scheme?"

Tyler shrugged his shoulders. "Well, if you must know, sir," he said with resignation, "I haven't one."

"Haven't one, hey? What's the idea, then, of all this folderol? I'd give a thousand dollars right now to be in the club."

"All this folderol, as you so accurately term one of the subtlest, indeed, I may say *the* subtlest, scheme that ever was hatched——"

"Tyler, don't beat about the bush. A child can see that you are up to something. But all this business of no food and no tobacco and, damn it, no sleep, is childish."

"Nerves, Mr Secretary, nerves," Tyler soothed him. "The basis of American civilization, sir. The basis, I may say, of American diplomacy. Time, sir, as you know, is the fourth dimension. It's the only dimension known to diplomacy. Just now we haven't got much time so I'm trying to manufacture it. The best way I know of manufacturing time is to be bored. I'm getting everybody so bored that sooner or later they'll lose patience and do something which will save

me the bother of thinking. If you will remember, sir,"
he continued, " that was the method you used to put
over your well-known polylateral treaty for the re-
duction of other people's battleships."

" If you mean that procrastination saved me any
thought, young man," the Secretary grumbled, " you're
a bigger fool than I thought you were."

" And if you think that I'm not thinking right now,"
Tyler retorted, " you——" He paused suggestively.

" Hmm ! " was the Secretary's only comment.

He stalked across the hall and pulled open the door
leading to the reception room. He turned.

" And if you don't finish your life in jail, young
man," he concluded, " it won't be for anything you
haven't done."

The door slammed shut.

" Hmm ! " Tyler mimicked. " And that's the man
whose career I'm saving. Well, well! Such is the
gratitude of republics. Next time I'm going to pick
out a nice little kingdom where a diplomat isn't
treated as a mixture of a sissy and an office-seeker.

" Just the same," he added. " I'd a damn sight
rather work for that senile old buccaneer than for all
the belted earls in Downing Street."

The coast was again clear. The Ambassador was

sitting implacably by the telephone, while the minutes of Lord Robert's life ticked relentlessly away. Murray and Peggy were in the garden. Acorn was playing poker. Urquhart was still encoding the fateful message to Tokio. Tyler smiled grimly as he thought what would happen to that telegram the moment it reached the Western Union Office. If Nichols had played his part according to instructions, Tyler foresaw that there would be some tall explanations in order on Monday morning. It was tricky work holding up diplomatic messages but the company could always discharge the ' responsible ' employee and hire him back again when it all blew over.

Tyler crept up the stairs, tread by tread, making as little noise as possible. The guard by the front door watched him with eyes as incurious as those of the bronze Buddha by the stairs. Half-way up Dennis paused, startled. A sudden whir, and the great clock that stood on the landing began to strike, slowly, inevitably, the ten strokes announcing the shortness of the time remaining. From below, Tyler could hear the Secretary's voice dinning over the telephone : " No, not M as in Moses but N as in Norris, J as in Johnson, K as in Kellogg, A as in Adams, G as in Gann——"

Once he had rounded the turn of the banisters,

Tyler moved more swiftly. He glanced hastily up and down the dimly lighted corridor. There was still a glimmer of light outside, and in the garden he could see a blur of white where the doomed diplomat was spending his last hours with a girl. Tyler tiptoed to the room where the safe was, a tall narrow iron box, coffin-shaped, with a single nickel knob gleaming in the light that slatted in through the shutters from the arc-lights in the street outside. He touched the knob and twirled it. As he did so, a little bluish bulb flashed on over the safe.

"Damn!" said Tyler. "Electric control!" He turned the knob back slowly until the light went off again. He would have to be careful. He needed help for a job like this. There was nothing for it but to call Robert.

He tiptoed down the corridor to the end of the wing, opened a window and whistled. As soon as an answering whistle told him that he had attracted the young diplomat's attention, he beckoned to Murray and ducked back out of sight. He returned to the little room with the safe and waited. As soon as Murray's steps sounded outside he went to the door.

"Watch out!" he said. "Let me know if you hear anyone coming. I'm going to open this safe!"

Lord Robert was surprised. " I say, Dennis," he protested, " are you quite sure you ought to ? "

" Rot! It's the only thing to do. I've got to find the switch for this electric control."

The safe was one of those innocent-looking devices in which a slight current is utilized to magnetize the working parts, thus making it impossible to work the combination. Any shift from neutral turned on the current and at the same time flashed on a light. Another light, as it happened in Urquhart's office, also flashed from the same current, while a third flashed in the hall. Unless Dennis could find the switch which controlled the current, his attempt to solve the combination would be useless.

" Wait ! " he whispered. " I hear some one coming ! "

The two men had barely time to hide behind the tall curtains which concealed the locked door communicating with the next room—the room where lay the body of the Prince—before Urquhart hurried into the room, flashed on the switch by the door and flooded the room with light. Peering through a slit in the curtain, his eyes narrowed to prevent reflection of the light from his eyeballs, Dennis watched Urquhart. Perspiration was starting from the Press Adviser's

forehead. He glanced swiftly round, went to the corner of the room farthest from the safe, and lifted a picture. He seemed to be satisfied. He let the picture slip back into place, turned out the light, and left the room.

" It's all right, your Excellency," they heard him call, as he went down the stairs. " It must have been Kanehira's imagination. I'll find Tyler."

Tyler waited a bare second for Urquhart to disappear and then kneeled down and removed his shoes. Moving noiselessly in his socks, he went directly to the corner where Urquhart had lifted the picture. His fingers groped over the dusty wall in the dark. In a moment they struck something. He fumbled with it. It was round and smooth and had the cold feel of metal. The switch! He tried it, nervously. It didn't bend and efforts to turn it were useless. Finally, he pulled. It came out smoothly with a little click. The current was off!

He turned back to the safe and groped for the combination. As he did so his fingers came in contact with a human hand, tense and moist. It was Lord Robert, already at work.

" No new thing to me, Dennis," was the Englishman's whispered comment. " Reminds me of the end

of the War, that time we burgled the German Consulate at Stockholm! "

The two men hung desperately against the safe, moving the tumblers slowly back and forth, straining their ears for the faint click that would tell of progress. Back and forth, first to the left, round and round and round. No result. Then to the right, slowly, clockwise, once, twice, thrice, a faint click rewarded them.

" You take it! " Robert whispered, " I'm going to file my fingers."

Tyler turned the knob delicately counter-clockwise. His willpower forced his consciousness into the tips of his fingers. It was useless. His fingers were wet with perspiration and felt hot and swollen. Murray had stooped and was rubbing his fingers hard on the window-ledge back and forth against the rough stone, until they were almost raw.

" Here! " he whispered. " Let me try again! "

The young diplomat's fingers were throbbing with pain. Glued to the little knob, they suddenly seemed to extend their nerves into the heart of the mechanism. Robert could feel the little tumblers shift and settle. Another little click shot through him with a pang. *The second tumbler was engaged.*

There was a flash and the little blue light over the

safe winked on again. Dennis leaped to the wall, swung the picture aside, groped for the switch. He found it. It had settled back into place. It must operate on some time attachment. He pulled it out again vigorously, and the light winked out.

"Wait!" he whispered tensely. "It will take a minute or so for the magnetism to drain out of that lock."

They waited, while the seconds ticked themselves leadenly away. Out in the garden they could hear voices. Downstairs all was quiet, though the woodwork was creaking round them and the noises of an old house were all about—sudden little ticks in the walls, slight quivers as the passage of a heavy bus shook the foundations.

"It's all right now," Tyler said, and they returned to their work. The last tumbler proved difficult to engage. Again and again they almost had it, again and again it refused to fall into the combination. So absorbed were they that they did not notice a silent figure which crept along the hall in the shadows and watched them for a moment through the half-open door. It hurried away. The house creaked and ticked on. Dennis went back to the switch and pulled it out once more, before it could turn on the current again.

"I think I'm getting it," Murray panted. "The thing is to turn on after the second click before turning it back."

"Listen!" Dennis exclaimed.

There was a sudden patter of footsteps across the hall and then the scream of a woman, agonized, in mortal terror.

"My God!" Robert gasped. "It's Peggy!"

The scream rang out again.

Murray straightened up and made for the door.

Dennis seized his arm. "Don't!" he begged and clung to the frantic young diplomat. "Don't you see?" he urged. "That's what they *want*. To get you away from here. The safe, man! Open it! It's our only chance. It's that or . . ."

VIII

THE ALTERNATIVE

A WORD went whispering over the wires of the world. Editors glanced wearily at the message on a flimsy yellow slip, then reached for telephones and ordered the presses to be stopped for a new edition. Wireless operators picked it up on ships far out at sea. They did not hesitate to wake the captain and give him the message at once. In a dozen Government offices men in uniform began checking over lists of ships, fuel, supplies. . . .

A group of little yellow men, wearing top hats, spectacles, and funereal frock-coats took a train to Nagasaki, raced on a fast cruiser across a yeasty yellow sea to Tientsin. There they took a special train to Peiping, where they spent the better part of a week talking very earnestly and smiling most urbanely at another group of smooth-faced little men. Another group, on yet another cruiser, raced northward across the same yeasty sea to Dairen, from which special trains carried them very rapidly for several days at high speed over a singularly flat and uninteresting country. At last they reached a large city,

filled with churches whose domes swelled unashamed
as the breasts of an Eastern princess.

At Washington the President announced that the
recent manœuvres in the Caribbean had clearly shown
that the fleet needed more cruisers, submarines, aircraft-carriers, and flotilla leaders, and he recom-
mended resumption of the 1930 programme. Pacifists
naturally protested that this would show that America
put all too little faith in the Kellogg Pact. So the
proposal was dropped. In London a Cabinet Minister
casually announced that in order to stimulate employ-
ment it had been decided to resume naval construction
work at Devonport. A number of elderly gentlemen
boarded steamers at Southampton and New York and
turned up in Washington and London respectively,
where they spent most of their time talking purpose-
fully to other elderly gentlemen. In various obscure
little islands a number of individuals disappeared
abruptly and without a word of explanation.

There was an insurrection in Bengal. There was a
revolution in Mexico. There were unemployment riots
in a score of European and American cities. Police-
men charged howling mobs of excited men, cracking
skulls, arresting the wrong people. Then a group of
California fruit-planters lynched a Chinese labourer

for what the papers termed a " sex offence," and the
Asiatic Press became very much excited. Then the
Moscow police shot three American and two British
newspaper correspondents for " capitalistic espionage,"
and the Anglo-Saxon Press became very much excited.
Then the Filipinos rose in revolt and an American
cruiser seized a Japanese freighter on the high seas off
Luzon. The ship was laden with ammunition for the
insurgents and there were a great many offers to
arbitrate.

Finally, the Japanese Chargés d'Affaires at London
and Washington, smiling with the utmost politeness,
simultaneously presented the Foreign Office and the
State Department with long identical notes, couched
in exquisite English, which made certain pointed re-
quests and intimated the necessity of receiving an
answer inside twenty-four hours. A tense Prime
Minister stood up that night before the House of
Commons and announced amid cheers that considera-
tions of national honour rendered it impossible for
Britain to desert her American kinsfolk in their hour
of need, and a group of hard-faced, grizzled men in
the Admiralty gave the radio operator a single word
which was flashed to his Majesty's ships on the seven
seas. . . . In Washington a perplexed and perspiring

President summoned his Cabinet to a midnight conference and argued at great length over whether the Monroe Doctrine applied to the Philippine Islands or whether self-defence was enough. Three hours later his speech had been mimeographed and sent to the newspaper offices for release not earlier than noon on the following day. The next morning he went before a joint session of the Houses of Congress and explained that for several highly moral reasons America found herself unexpectedly in a state of war. . . .

A sailor on the *Pensacola* saw a smudge of smoke on the western horizon. A few minutes later a plane was catapulted into the air and sent roaring and dwindling in the direction of the smoke. Half an hour later the plane came back in a hurry. The Japanese fleet was in sight. The two fleets strung out on converging lines to the north of the islands. A distant flash and rumble, a roar like an express train, a pillar of water fountaining up five hundred yards beyond the ship. More flashes and splashes. The reeling shock of a broadside. The staggering blow of a direct hit. Seaplanes, bombs, torpedoes. Darkness. What was left of the American fleet that night returned to Pearl Harbour, where it remained for three months undergoing repairs. What was left of the Japanese fleet

crawled back to Guam, content to have secured the Pacific flank of the Philippines.

Cruisers playing round the islands sank ships, wrecked cable and wireless stations. Ships were sunk by bombs, by torpedoes, by shell-fire. Seven cruisers were wrecked in the terrible storm that swept over Melanesia that season. . . .

War. A Minnesota boy drove his bayonet into the stomach of a little yellow man in a Luzon jungle. . . . A submarine commander fired a torpedo at a transport crowded with seasick American soldiers. . . . A British intelligence officer faced a firing squad at Samarkand with a smile on his lips. . . . Women received tele-grams which turned them old. . . . Casualty lists. . . . Higher prices. . . . Crushing taxation. . . . Riveters and welders in shipyards, blast furnaces flaring in Pittsburgh, flags on pulpits. Suicides. . . . A bomb exploded in the Executive Offices at Washington. A Private Secretary was killed, but the President (thank God!) had left a minute earlier to be photographed for the talking pictures in conversation with the British Ambassador. . . .

The American fleet made its epoch-making move. After destroying all means of communication on the Hawaiian Islands the fleet steamed south-by-east,

cruisers, destroyers, aircraft-carriers, and battleships. A thousand miles west of Panama was the first rendezvous with tankers, for refuelling. The course continued southward to the Falkland Islands. Fuelling once more, the fleet stood eastward toward Australia. Five hundred miles south of Cape Town fresh tankers from Newport News met it, with more ammunition, more destroyers, and another aircraft-carrier. A few days later the fleet steamed into the roadstead at Singapore, having gone three-fourths of the way round the world and effected a junction with the British fleet before the Japanese cruisers patrolling the Western Pacific realized that Hawaii was unguarded. . . .

Two days later the combined fleets steamed southeasterly across the China Sea, established an advanced base on Mindanao and then organized a bridge-head on Luzon. There was fighting in Luzon. Manila lay in ruins. Behind the fleet came the transports, with men and guns and planes, from Australia, from Canada and America, from England and from South Africa. The Japanese raid on Hong-Kong and the battle of Formosa, when Japan ceased to exist as a first-class naval Power. Submarines in the Yellow Sea, freighters and transports plunging downward as the underwater war systematically gnawed away the bridge of ships

between Japan and the mainland. China paralysed by fresh revolts and indefatigable factions; the Indian revolution was languishing. The great Russian army was wiped out in the battle of the Khyber Pass and the retreat through Afghanistan.

The war stopped. No one quite knew why. Nobody knew who had won or lost. Two hundred thousand men had died, principally as a result of disease, and as many more wounded. For a generation the economic progress of the entire Basin of the Pacific had been definitely blasted. For another year the Eastern Mediterranean was rocked as Italy tried to collect what the Allies had promised. After the serious reverses at Alexandretta had checked the Italian campaign, that war drifted into a stalemate and a happy compromise was found by turning the French mandate of Syria over to Rome. That year the famine in Russia led to a decline of Soviet influence—three million people having starved to death in the Ukraine alone. Germany denounced its treaty with Moscow and joined the Anglo-American alliance, it being understood that there would be no more reparations. France, facing the fate of a second-class Power, signed a treaty of alliance with Moscow, where it was welcomed with cynical impotence. And the old game went on.

During these troubled years, it is pleasant to report, the League of Nations settled the dispute over the boundary between the Republic of Brazil and Dutch Guiana, supervised a plebiscite in Slovakia and drafted no less than seven international treaties (none of which were subsequently ratified). At the close of the war all nations reaffirmed their faith in the Kellogg Pact, and the Permanent Court of International Justice at The Hague handed down its famous decision regarding the Glotzheimer Concession in the case brought by Costa Rica against Poland. . . .

SECOND FLOOR OF EMBASSY

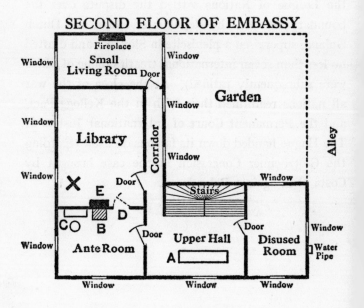

A. Couch where Peggy hid.
B. Safe.
C. Table and chair.
D. Doorway concealed behind curtains.
E. Fireplace.
X. Where the body was found.

PART III

TORTURE ON TAP

PEGGY crouched in the shadows of the upstairs corridor, watching, flattened against the wall so that the light from the hall passed her, like a thrown knife which has missed its mark. Downstairs she heard the shuffling of feet and the low grumble of men's voices. Once she started with fright, as Urquhart appeared suddenly, walking silently in his tennis shoes. Her heart pounded madly. She was too late to warn Murray. She watched breathless, as the Press Adviser strode swiftly into the little anteroom. She waited for the outcry which would announce his discovery of the men at the safe. All was silence. In a few moments Urquhart reappeared, glanced thoughtfully to right and to left, and then went swiftly downstairs.

Her position would not do. By the time she saw anyone coming they would be nearer the anteroom than she. She could not warn her lover in time. Where should she go? Then she thought of the divan opposite the head of the stairs, where Dennis had slept the night before. If she hid behind that she would be able to see whoever came up the stairs. She

knelt down in the wedge of shadow and removed her shoes. That would be better, more silent. She hesitated. The silk of her stockings might catch on a splinter in the flooring and betray her with the thin, sharp sound of rending silk. She unrolled her stockings and stripped them off, delicately, so that the rustle wouldn't be heard. She tiptoed softly round the corner and found herself alone in the upper hall. There was just room behind the couch for her to crouch unseen. She could watch the stairs from beneath it, through the legs.

Kanehira, that was the man Robert had told her to watch; she would wait for him here, where she could see him long before he neared the room with the safe. Peggy knew now that Kanehira was guilty. He was a Japanese valet and they are always the ones who are discovered in the last reel to have plunged the crinkly knife into the old gentleman's back. There could be no doubt about it, Kanehira *must* have done it. She had suspected him from the moment she saw him. Intuition. Why, it was perfectly obvious. Anybody would know that a man like Robert wouldn't kill anybody when there was a horrid slinky little Oriental valet around to do the job.

Again she stiffened with fright. There had been a

little creak on the stairs. Peering from the shadows, she saw a yellow, wedge-shaped face, impassive, sly. It was Kanehira. She was about to call out when suddenly she hesitated. She had never thought of that. If she called now she would alarm the Embassy and have everybody come upstairs. She couldn't do that. The thing she should have done was to have got up and sat on the sofa and looked natural. Then the next time Kanehira came she could have given him an order, sent him downstairs for a glass of ice-water; and if it were Urquhart, she could have asked him to sit down and talk to her for a little because she was bored. Why hadn't she thought of that before? Of course, now she would have to wait until Kanehira went away. She wished . . .

It was too late. Kanehira was in the hall, walking silently as a yellow cat, walking oddly, walking in a semicircle so that the hall light would not throw his shadow toward the door of the anteroom. He edged round until at one time he was so close that Peggy could have reached from under the sofa and laid her hand on the heavy grey cotton socks with which he had muffled his shoes. Now he had won to a little patch of shadow which would cover his advance toward the anteroom. He crouched by the door, listening

intently as the two dim figures within worked and whispered at the lock of the tall safe, the safe that somehow resembled a coffin.

Peggy felt that she could stand it no longer. She felt that she must scream, throw something, do anything to warn the men inside the room of the doom which was at the door. Swiftly and unexpectedly Kanehira turned away. His face was grey with terror. He retreated, again silently following the circle which kept his shadow from falling toward the door of the anteroom. Again he passed so close that Peggy could have touched him. Now he had crept to the head of the stairs. He slipped silently down them. By peering over the top of the sofa she was able to watch him down to the turn of the landing.

Now was her chance to slip out from behind the divan and to follow her new strategy! She was too late. Frank Urquhart was coming up the stairs. Kanehira was waiting for him at the landing. She saw the valet speaking, hurriedly and earnestly, to the Press Secretary and saw Urquhart's face turn suddenly haggard and old. She guessed what he had heard. Urquhart answered softly, vehemently. Kanehira nodded once, turned and ran rapidly down the stairs and out of sight.

Peggy crouched down again as Urquhart continued to climb, making no noise. On his face there was an expression of indescribable horror. He looked like a man who was struggling with a walking nightmare, he looked as though he were at grips with something old and evil and infinitely dangerous. He looked afraid.

The girl strangled a scream as the harrowed face came closer and closer. Then the angle of the sofa cut it off; all she could see was a begrimed silk shirt, then a belt, then flannel trousers, and finally socks and rubber-soled shoes. She watched those shoes with terror. And all this time Urquhart made no noise.

With a pang of relief she saw that he had turned away from the anteroom and was walking silently toward a little room on the opposite side of the hall. Then with a blinding flash of intuition she knew that he was running away. She could no longer see his eyes bulging with terror and his forehead dewed with sweat, but the furtive and irresolute padding of his feet she *could* see, and they told their story. Now he had left the hall and had entered the little room.

Again Peggy straightened up. Something was about to happen. She followed him, walking quietly, avoiding the cast of her shadow as Kanehira had done.

The door of the room where Urquhart was stood half
open, as if to let him hear any noise of pursuit. Through
it she could see, hung like a picture in the darkened
room, a square blue-black piece of the night sky,
framed in a window, criss-crossed with iron bars. As
she watched, a hand was silhouetted against the bars.
The hand fumbled for a moment and then the bars
swung silently open, like a door. That side of the
building, she remembered, would be in shadow, as the
arc-lights were diagonally opposite the other side of
the Embassy. It must be a sheer twenty-foot drop
into the alley, but an active man might be able to
lessen the danger of a fall by clinging, for a yard or
two, to the rough brickwork and the vines. And if he
knew the trick of falling he need not be hurt. As
Peggy watched, the black bulk of a body blotted out
the night sky. Urquhart was crawling through the
window. Actuated by some impulse she could not
explain, she abandoned all caution. She ran forward
and grabbed him, as he lay across the sill, half out of
the room. She did not think to look if there were
anything behind her. As she touched the man in the
window, a black shadow flickered in front of her eyes
like a bat and the soft caress of a silk scarf at her
throat tightened like the lash of a whip, stranglingly.

She collapsed on the floor, her fingers clawing desperately at the grip of the silent terror which was throttling her. Mercifully, she fainted. . . .

Urquhart had seen the second flash of the telltale light in the hall below, as the current was earthed through the safe for the second time. So there *was* some one at the safe and Kanehira's tale *was* correct. He had started, intending to investigate more thoroughly this time, walking quietly so as not to disturb whoever was at work. He had had no doubts it was Tyler. If he caught him it would be a nasty scandal. On the landing, however, he had met Kanehira, who had stammered a few words into his ear. It was not what the valet had seen that alarmed him. He knew the safe and the combination and doubted if anyone short of an expert cracksman could master that last queer double turn. But the mention of the Black Dragons had sent an icy blast of terror through him. It was unlucky even to think of them, let alone mention them. Urquhart thought with sick horror of what the Dragons had done to a little man in Kyoto who had betrayed one of their number to the police. He could still see the wretch writhing in the blood-smeared agony of the Way of the Thousand Slices.

Urquhart knew he need expect no mercy. There was
no quarter in that war. He forgot everything in the
memory of what the Dragons did when their plans
miscarried. If only he had never sworn that oath—
he had done it for a jest, really, that time in Tokio. . . .
And now Kanehira had demanded help in the Black
Dragon's name. Curse these Oriental institutions!

All that Urquhart knew was that he must escape,
somehow and at once. He must win clear from the
Embassy. He would take the first train south. He
knew a moonshiner in the Tennessee mountains who
would protect him. Not even the American Government could reach him there. Later, perhaps, he could
explain things, but now he must get away. He went
quietly upstairs and tiptoed into the little room. He
tried the catch on the bars of the window, a trick he
had accidentally discovered a year before. If you only
knew where to press, the entire frame swung out
like a door, a vagary of the Counsellor of Embassy
who had gone mad from overwork during the War
and fancied that he was being pursued by Mexican
assassins, before he was detected and sent back to
Tokio.

Ah, that was it! The catch still worked. He
hoisted himself slowly on to the window-ledge and

peered out. Yes, there they were, in the shadow by the copper water-pipe, that series of little projecting iron hooks by which you could climb to the ground, hidden by the shadow. Below him lay the cobbled alley, opposite him a blank wall. He looked round to see if the coast was clear. Damn! Almost directly below, an alternating red spark flared and paled, as somebody puffed at a cigar. There was some one in the alley! The police? The Secret Service men who keep watch on all foreign missions? A passer-by? A darky waiting for his sweetheart?

Urquhart gave a violent start. A hand clutched at his shoulder. He bit his tongue in an effort to restrain himself and turned with an explanation on his lips. The hand was abruptly withdrawn. He found himself confronting Kanehira, who was twisting a frail silk scarf round the throat of a prostrate girl.

Urquhart was cornered. He thought desperately to evolve a new line of action. He struck Kanehira's hand away with feverish haste, closed the door silently and swiftly, and then turned back to the girl. Stooping over her, he bound her hands firmly with the scarf with which Kanehira had started to garotte her. Then he faced Kanehira.

"Tie me up!" he ordered in a hoarse whisper.

Obediently, the valet bound his hands loosely with Urquhart's own tie.

" Listen! " Urquhart whispered, as Kanehira bent low. " We must save time, keep them away from that safe until the telegram has been sent. You can't get away now. There's a man down in the alley. You've gone mad, do you see? Your brain has been turned with grief for the loss of your master, murdered by a white man. You've decided to take your revenge on the race who murdered Prince Hojo. You've caught us and now you're going to torture us. Got that? You begin on the girl. That will work. What happens later doesn't matter very much. I'll think of something. Now we've got to gain time. That's the scenario. Got it? "

Kanehira nodded. He went to the wall and pressed a button. The room was flooded with light. He looked round him. Then he saw something which pleased him, an electric lamp with a cord for connexions. He ripped the cord from the lamp, separated the two wires, taking care not to injure the insulation, and plugged the cord in at a wall connexion. He then put one of the wires against the bare foot of the unconscious girl. Diffidently, he brought the other wire close to the other foot. The torture was beginning.

Peggy came to her senses with a sickening plunge of horror and a stab of pain. She gazed wildly round. She saw the valet, his face contorted in a death's-head grin, bending over her.

" You kill my master," Kanehira chuckled mirthlessly. " You die. You die, not slowly, yes? "

She craned her neck away to avoid the evil leer on the servant's face. He was mad, she could tell, by the way he talked and the wild light in his eyes. She then saw Urquhart lying bound in the other corner. The man smiled ruefully.

" Keep up your courage," he whispered. " Help can't be far off."

" Help! " she screamed, as the current again burned her feet, contorting her with a paroxysm of pain.

Kanehira smiled. " Now I make you no see," he remarked, in a perfectly conversational voice.

She thrashed round to elude him, but it was pitifully useless. She screamed for help once more, before the man's hand was clapped over her mouth and her shriek was stifled.

Kanehira crouched down and clasped her head between his knees, as in a vice. He held one wire firmly against her cheek, while, with the other, he reached for her eyes. She closed them to shut out the

vision, but a thumb sought for and pressed back her eyelid. Ignoring her struggles, he forced the bare end of the other wire nearer and nearer her eyeball. In a moment the power of a hundred and ten volts would blast her eyesight. Then everything went black and the world was plunged in the unplumbed darkness of the blind.

II

THE GOD FROM THE FRIGIDAIRE

YES, boys," boomed Acorn jovially, "this is much more like it. Four kings are very, very hard to beat."

By this time, with the aid of a stripped deck and wild deuces, the Assistant Secretary had somewhat redressed the balance against him. There was no question but that the cards were coming his way. Joe O'Connor, the bootlegger, might have told him a little about how it happened that the Assistant Secretary's hands were invariably better than the best either of the others held. O'Connor was a diplomat himself, in his own way, and he had a feeling in his bones that it was not very lucky to trim one of the big shots of the State Department. If it wasn't for a coupla Senators and a Federal Judge or so, O'Connor mused, he mighta taken a trip to Atlanta with the rest of the boys that time they got the new enforcement guy that wasn't wise. Bill Strong was mercifully ignorant of the dipso-diplomacy of his colleague, guessed the cards weren't sitting right that night, bet his hands lightly—he had a hundred of Acorn's money salted away

which was never going to see its old home again—and drank.

He drank and drank. They were all drinking. The gnawing of the desire for nicotine, he found, was somewhat dulled by plenty of Scotch. For that matter, he asked himself, what wasn't? Strong was, for Strong, rather tipsy. That is to say, his face was redder than usual, he played his hands very close to his chest, did everything deliberately, and spoke so slowly that every one but himself forgot the beginning of his remarks before he had concluded them.

" Five aces! " Acorn remarked proudly. " Pity you boys wouldn't bet with me. That's another round of roodles."

Joe O'Connor's little eyes shifted from one to the other of his companions. He guessed Strong was wise. Why wouldn't he have bid up on five queens if he wasn't on?

Strong picked up the whisky-bottle and tilted it over his glass. Only a few pallid amber drops trickled out.

" That . . . hair-tonic . . . of yours . . . Joe," he observed, spacing his words as far apart as telegraph-poles, " is . . . great . . . for . . . chilblains." He stopped and, as no one laughed, smiled with condescending bitterness.

" Guess . . . we'd . . . better . . . have . . . another bottle! "

" Nonsense," the Under-Secretary grumbled. He had just picked up a straight flush. " We don't want any more."

" Oh . . . yes . . . we . . . do," Strong gradually proclaimed. " I'll . . . get . . . another . . . bottle. . . . Won't . . . play . . . this . . . hand . . . anyhow. . . . The . . . cards . . . aren't . . . coming . . . my . . . way . . . any . . . more."

" For God's sake, then, hurry up! " Acorn settled back to an exchange of bets with O'Connor, who had figured to a cent the precise amount he was going to lose to the Under-Secretary that hand.

" Raise you five! "

" See you five and raise you five! "

Strong shambled back to the kitchen, selected with becoming gravity one of the surviving bottles of bootleg, uncorked it and sampled it. He returned to the poker game, poured generous drinks all round, observing the principle that charity begins at home. Acorn swirled his drink round his glass and sampled it.

" Hey! " he protested. " This stuff is lukewarm. We ought to have some ice."

" I'll . . . get . . . ice . . ." Strong offered.

" You'll stay here." This time Acorn held a full house, aces over kings. " Where's that Jap, anyhow? He ought to bring us the ice. Hey there, boy! "

" He's . . . not . . . out . . . in . . . the . . . kitchen. . . . I . . . can . . . tell . . . you . . . that . . . much! "

Acorn glared about him judicially. Things had come to a pretty pass when a poker game had to be broken up in order to get ice for the drinks.

" You go and look for him, Strong," he decided at last. " The hands will keep."

Strong lurched a little and had to catch the wall to regain his balance. The heat, he reflected, was trying. In another ten minutes he would go to sleep, but he still had that hundred dollars. Leaving behind him a protracted confession that he did not intend to bet on that hand anyhow, he departed to a brisk murmur of bets.

In the kitchen he found himself face to face with a full whisky-bottle and some glasses, a challenge Bill Strong had never been known to refuse. He felt weak and dizzy and utterly disgusted. If he ever got out of this dump he'd see to it that the Japanese Embassy never got a break in the news for ever after. He——— Oh, hell!—what was the use? Not a damned thing to do but get drunk. He poured himself a half-tumbler

full of the warmish whisky and drained it with the swallowless single gulp of the trained toper. Ought he to have done that on an empty stomach?

A moment later the question was answered for him. He found himself lying on the floor of the kitchen, staring vaguely at the large and glittering frigidaire. Le's see! What . . . had . . . he . . . come . . . there . . . for? He racked his aching head. Ice! That . . . was . . . it. The men in the poker game wanted ice. Well, Bill Strong would show 'em that when he went for ice he came back with ice. What . . . was . . . that? Sounded . . . like . . . a . . . woman . . . hollering . . . no. . . . Ice! . . . tha's . . . the . . . stuff. . . . Ice!

He seized the nickel-plated handle of the ice-box and pulled. Funny it didn't open. He pulled hard, instead of lifting the handle. Still it didn't open. He pulled again. The cabinet slid forward a few inches from the wall. Perhaps it opened in the back. Never . . . could . . . tell . . . 'bout . . . these damned . . . foreigners. He looked at the back. There was no sign of an opening. There! Down by the bottom there was some sort of string. Perhaps it would open if he pulled that. He seized the electric cord which supplied the power for the frigidaire and pulled. The damned thing would not budge. To hell with it, anyhow! He took a firm

grip and jerked with all his might. The base-plug
ripped clear with a shower of sparks as the current
short-circuited. There was a flash and then the lights
went out, as the fuses burned out with a splutter and a
crackle behind the little isinglass windows. . . .

"Hey there!" Acorn's roar of anguish was a terrible thing to hear. He had just picked up the best
hand he had ever held in his life, when the lights
failed. The Embassy lay plunged in darkness. And
Strong lay at the foot of the frigidaire, dead to the
world.

THE MAN IN THE SAFE

THE scream died away into silence. Murray paused again, his throbbing fingers glued to the metal knob of the safe.

"Damn it!" he insisted. "I *shall* go. It's Peggy!"

"You can't," Tyler repeated. "This thing is too serious now. It's bigger than even her need for you."

Silently the young diplomat resumed his play with the tumblers. They clicked finally into place. He twirled the knob back. The combination held. He seized the handle and pressed up, then down. It moved stiffly downward, until it pointed at a sharp angle. Downstairs there was a slamming of doors and the sound of running feet. Then suddenly the light went out in the hall outside. The Embassy was plunged in darkness. Murray let his hand drop from the handle of the safe. Its door swung slowly open and a man leaped out upon him.

In a moment the two men found themselves engaged in a confused and desperate struggle in the dark, and the room seemed suddenly full of people. Kanehira, followed closely by Urquhart, burst in and fell upon Dennis.

Tyler found himself thrashing round on the floor as the little valet fought with the fury of a trapped animal. He had no idea of what was happening to Murray, having heard only a gasp as the young Englishman struggled with the silent figure from the safe. He had no time for thought. Kanehira had struck him a sharp blow on the shoulder and his entire left arm had gone numb. He could feel the valet's thumb pressing in, fumbling for that nerve which means death in jiujitsu. A thrill of agonizing pain ran through him. He twisted his shoulder away, but the thumb still bored in mercilessly.

Suddenly he heard a strangled cry of disgust and horror. "My God! He's dead!"

At the words Kanehira tore himself loose from Tyler's grip and darted for the door, but he was too late; Murray had straightened up just in time to tackle the fleeing valet. Tyler had a chance to think.

"Now's the time!" He exulted. "The Black Dragon trick." Circling the group on the floor, he bent low and called the password of the secret order.

"Togo!"

Was his hunch correct? He strained for an answer. For a moment there was only the hoarse panting of the

combatants. Then the answer came, in the clipped metallic accent of Japan.

" Goto! "

His triumph was brief. There was the thud of a heavy blow, a short moan, and then silence. He felt, rather than saw, a form steal silently to the door. Who had struck Kanehira? Murray? Urquhart?

" Thanks, old man," his friend called out. " That did for him."

So it was Urquhart. Tyler was about to rush to the door in pursuit of the fleeing Press Adviser, when, to his amazement, he heard the latter's voice in the hall outside, calling excitedly.

" Mr Ambassador! Can you come up? I've caught him ! "

There was a flicker of candlelight in the hall below and the sound of steps coming up the stairs. The Ambassador and the Secretary of State, alarmed by the tumult upstairs, had already started up when the lights had failed. They had groped their steps to the reception room and had wrenched the candles from the tall sconces over the fireplace.

So it was that Dennis Tyler saw a weird vision of two old men, their faces seamed with wrinkles and their grey hair gleaming in the flickering candlelight,

mounting the stairs carrying long guttering tapers in their hands, like penitentials in a religious procession.

They marched slowly up the stairs, the candles guttering and the melted wax streaking grimly down the tapers. They entered the room, still silent, and held the candles out at arm's length, to inspect the gruesome spectacle on the floor. At their side stood Urquhart.

There stood Murray, his white clothes covered with dust and blood. At his feet sprawled the prostrate Kanehira, face down, his breath snoring in the spasms of concussion, a gaping wound in the back of his head, where a crushing blow had fallen. On the floor by the safe lay the instrument which had done it, the same brass poker with which the Prince had been murdered.

That was not all. Lying close to Kanehira was the naked body of another man, short and dark-skinned like the Japanese valet himself. Tyler reached over and touched him. He removed his fingers quickly.

"He's dead. Cold as ice," he commented.

He stooped again and lifted the arm of the naked man. It lifted stiffly, but not with the utter rigidity of the recent dead.

"He's been dead at least forty-eight hours," Tyler added thoughtfully, "*Rigor mortis* is passing."

" Who is he ? " demanded the Ambassador, in a low, tense voice.

Reluctantly, the Chief of the C.P.I. knelt down and turned the body over. While there was no mark, the protruding eyes and tongue showed that the man had been strangled.

Tyler studied the face.

" I don't know him," he said. " But he looks enough like Kanehira to be his brother ! "

" Kanehira ! " the Ambassador exclaimed. " Kanehira had no brother ! "

The old diplomat moved closer and held the candle over the face of the corpse. In the play of light and shadow it looked as though the dead man were grimacing at them. A drop of wax fell from the candle with an ugly little plop on to the pitiful tortured face that stared up at them. Another drop fell and then another. The Ambassador's hand was shaking.

" It *is* Kanehira ! " he said at last.

The Secretary muttered something savagely, under his breath.

Viscount Kondo turned and pointed at the unconscious valet. " Then who is *he* ? " he demanded harshly.

" Hiki ! " It was Urquhart who had spoken.

Every face turned to the Press Adviser.

"Yes," Urquhart repeated, "Hiki, the actor. If you will listen to me, your Excellency, I can explain everything——"

IV

IN THE DARK

THE Ambassador blinked once and nodded. "Proceed," he ordered, tonelessly.

"This is goin' to be good," was Tyler's unspoken comment.

"For some time," Urquhart began, "it had been evident to me that Lord Robert had succeeded completely in pulling the wool over Mr Tyler's eyes. I don't blame Mr Tyler for that. Lord Robert is entirely plausible. He is a close friend of Mr Tyler's. Mr Tyler has been in a very difficult position and I feel sorry for him."

"Never mind my feelin's," Tyler assured him. "What we want is—ah!—justice."

"It had never occurred to me that Lord Robert had an accomplice. I had been watching Kanehira. I felt that the shock of Prince Hojo's death might well have unsettled his reason and that he might consider some sort of revenge possible. I have spent many years in Japan, your Excellency, and I know the deep reverence which every loyal Japanese has for the Imperial Family. To speak frankly, I was afraid that Kanehira

might feel that it was his duty to take matters into his own hands, particularly as his late master had been, so to speak, under his express care. It had never occurred to me that Kanehira was an impostor. What I had thought was grief was desperation, a desire to escape. I ought to thank Mr Tyler for having been clever enough at the very outset to set a guard on the Embassy. It prevented the escape of the criminals."

"Thank you," murmured the Chief of the C.P.I.

"No sarcasm, please, Tyler," snapped the Secretary of State. "I want to hear Urquhart."

Tyler looked his mute appeal at his Chief, but the latter ignored him.

"Well, then," Urquhart continued. "I felt reasonably sure that Lord Robert would attempt to escape. The telltale light in the hall showed me that he and Mr Tyler were engaged in tampering with the safe. I thought that was harmless enough, as it never occurred to me that he would succeed in opening it. As it turned out, he was setting a trap for his wretched accomplice, and presumably planned to escape in the confusion. A few minutes ago, I made the rounds to make sure that there was no way out. As I was looking out of the little window in the room across the hall, Miss Lawrence tried to drag me back. She, like Mr Tyler, believes in

Lord Robert's innocence and has been watching me. Lord Robert had entirely succeeded in diverting suspicion from himself to me. At that moment Kanehira attacked us. He caught me unawares and before I knew how he had contrived it he had bound us both. He seemed to have lost his mind and began torturing Miss Lawrence. I thought that with her first scream Tyler would come to her aid. For some reason he did not."

"Do you mean to tell me," Dennis demanded, running his hands energetically through his hair, "that Peggy Lawrence is still tied up?"

"My God," Urquhart exclaimed, "so she is!"

Without a word Dennis turned on his heel and left the room. Despite the darkness he found his way easily to the little room where Peggy lay, conscious again and, although she had received a severe shock, sufficiently recovered to be thoroughly angry.

"Keep a stiff upper lip, child," Dennis instructed her, as he untied her bonds. "I won't fail you. The C.P.I. never fails."

A minute later he had returned to the group in the candlelight, with Peggy beside him. She gasped when she saw the bodies on the floor, then raised her eyes and smiled shyly at her lover.

" Peggy," Tyler apologized, " this is no place for you, but before you go downstairs I ought to tell you that Frank Urquhart says that you caught him looking out of a window, that Kanehira attacked you both and tied you up and started torturing you. Is that correct?"

" That's right," she answered, " but I'm not going to leave. I—I—belong up here—with——" The tears started into her eyes and she turned her face away to conceal the working of her mouth.

" All right, Frank," Tyler informed the Press Adviser. " Continue with your entertainment."

" Suddenly the lights went out," Urquhart resumed his account. " By the time my eyes had become used to the darkness, I saw that Kanehira had left the room and I could hear a fight of some sort going on in this room."

" Quite right," Tyler corroborated. " It *was* a fight."

" I managed to work loose. Kanehira had not tied me as firmly as he thought. I followed him in here and was just in time to see Lord Robert Murray strike Kanehira from behind as he was struggling with Mr Tyler in front of the safe. Then the Secretary and the Ambassador arrived and I was able to explain at last the real situation."

There was a little pause.

" And what, Mr Urquhart," the Secretary inquired, " is the real situation ? "

" The real situation, Mr Secretary," Urquhart explained, " is appallingly simple. The man in the safe was, of course, the real Kanehira. The impostor who took his place was Hiki, the famous film star. Apparently Hiki was a British Secret Service agent as well as a very fine actor. Not knowing he was dealing with a madman in the person of Lord Robert Murray, he allowed himself to become involved in this discreditable venture. Probably he did not know, up to the last moment, that he was expected to kill Prince Hojo. He secreted himself in the Embassy, perhaps in this very room, and at the first opportunity he murdered Kanehira. There is no need to tell you how he did it. He strangled him, using the thuggee device which is common throughout Asia and which he tried on Miss Lawrence this evening."

The girl put her hand to her red and swollen throat and nodded. Despite her recent ordeal, she was tense with excitement.

" Hiki knew the combination of the safe. There is no need to inquire how he knew it. Lord Robert's facility in opening it in the dark is evidence of that. Hiki concealed the dead man in the safe and then

calmly put on Kanehira's clothes and went into Prince
Hojo's room. The windows were shuttered on account
of the heat. Hiki was the greatest character artist in
Japan and it was child's play for him to impersonate
the dead valet. He drugged the drinks—a neat touch
this, to divert suspicion from Lord Robert—and then
committed the murder he had been hired to perform.
I assume that it was only then he realized that it was
Prince Hojo he had killed. I very much doubt that
even a renegade Japanese could have been persuaded
to murder a member of the Imperial Family. I have
no doubt that Hiki was terror-stricken when he discovered the crime he had committed and made desperate efforts to escape. I will not attempt to explain
exactly how Lord Robert planned to make his escape
or what obscure motives prompted him to set his tool
to attack us. One thing is certain, however," Urquhart
concluded, " the British Chargé's plans did not include
the escape of his accomplice. He seized the opportunity to kill Hiki, thus destroying the one man who
could incriminate him."

Murray looked up hopefully. " I say, Tyler," he
said, " you can tell them that I didn't do that. I was
too busy fighting to sneak around and brain him with
a poker."

Dennis shook his head. " As a matter of fact," he said brightly, " nobody killed dear old Hiki. He's simply unconscious. He's got a nasty hole in the back of his head but he's not dead by a damned sight, and with a little expert surgery will live to testify at his own trial for murder. However, that won't help now.

" I must say," he continued, turning to Urquhart, " now that you've explained it all so cleverly I've got to apologize to you, Frank. I am free to admit, as you guessed, that I thought you were guilty. Lord knows I'm fond of Murray, but this isn't a time for sentiment. He knew that the Prince was coming and the rest you've worked out so neatly it would be a shame to argue with you. You've thought of everything and have an explanation for everything and the telegram's gone to Tokio and as soon as we've dealt with Murray I'm going home to order ten more large cruisers right away."

" Huh! " The Secretary's grunt of surprise was genuine. " That is the first time, Tyler," he remarked, with considerable satisfaction, " that I've ever known you to admit that you made a mistake."

Tyler turned vigorously and confronted his Chief. " This is no time for me to pride myself on my opinions," he explained. " I've made a mistake and I

hate to admit it, but this is serious. If it weren't for the Service, I'd resign at once."

Peggy started forward. " Oh, it's shameful! You can't condemn him this way, without a chance to speak a word in his defence."

Tyler walked up to his friend and eyed him steadily. Murray saw the left eyelid of the Chief of the C.P.I. flicker once, twice, unmistakably. " Well," demanded Tyler, " have you anything to say for yourself ? "

Lord Robert glared round wildly. " There's nothing to say," he objected. " Not one of you will believe me."

Tyler turned back to the girl. " You see, Peggy," he told her softly. " it's no use. He's practically given himself away. If he were innocent he'd have more to say than that. Keep your head," he added in a whisper, which the others could not hear. " The show's not over yet."

" Go downstairs," he ordered in a louder, kindly tone. " This is no place for you."

She left the room, sobbing hysterically, and collapsed on the sofa in the hall outside.

When Tyler returned, he found the Ambassador, the Secretary, and Urquhart conferring in low tones, while Murray stood defiantly watching them in the flickering candlelight.

" Come here, Tyler," the Secretary ordered. " What shall we do? "

" Perfectly simple," Tyler replied slowly. " Lord Robert is a gentleman. If we leave him here for a few minutes with a loaded revolver he will know what to do. We can make up an explanation later."

Urquhart nodded eagerly. " What about these dead men? " he demanded.

" You seem determined to have Hiki dead," Tyler commented. " Now, my dear old Frank, just *do* be reasonable. You can bury Kanehira in the cellar. Quick-lime is quite inexpensive and what's an Embassy without a corpse or so in the basement? As for Hiki, I suggest that he be given medical attention later and sent back to Japan. What happens to him there will be nobody's business. How does that strike your Excellency? " he added, turning to the Ambassador.

Viscount Kondo nodded. " That will do, Mr Tyler," he agreed.

Tyler left the group and strode across the room to where Murray was waiting in the shadows.

" Bob," said Tyler, his voice shaking with emotion, " it goes hard with me to do this but it is my duty. We are going to give you an opportunity to die like a gentleman. Urquhart is going downstairs for a sheet

H

of paper and a pen. As soon as he has returned, we will leave you in here for five minutes with a candle, a loaded revolver and the means of writing a confession. At the end of that period, you will have signed the confession and done what you know is called for by the circumstances.

" Do you agree ? " he concluded.

Murray's eyes travelled round the group, seeking for a sign of mercy. There was none. The Secretary of State looked grave and impassive. The Ambassador resembled nothing so much as Fate, in his stern relent-lessness. Urquhart was as elated as a prosecuting attorney who has got his verdict. Tyler was troubled and hopeless. Murray hesitated.

Finally he spoke and a gasp broke from his hearers as he ordered brusquely : " Bring the paper ! "

THE BLINDFOLD TEST

URQUHART fairly bounded from the room, exultation in his stride. It was a great feather in the Press Adviser's cap to have brought home the responsibility for a baffling crime to the British Chargé d'Affaires. Frank Urquhart knew now that he was 'fixed' for life; no Government would ever let him go unrewarded after such a *coup*. Paying no heed to the girl who had collapsed disconsolate on the sofa, Urquhart felt his way downstairs in the dark in search of paper and a fountain-pen.

When he was gone, Tyler turned to the Ambassador. "If you don't mind, sir," he suggested, "I'll shift this blighter"—pointing to the prostrate Hiki—"into another room. And as soon as this little ceremony is over, I suggest calling an ambulance and seeing what a surgeon can do to that skull of his. It looks like a simple case of trepanning and then you'll be able to hear his side of the story."

Viscount Kondo nodded and turned away. He felt very tired. The Secretary of State looked old and a little frightened. As Tyler lifted the head of the

cinema actor, the Secretary took his feet and together they carried the unconscious accomplice to the room at the far end of the wing and laid him on the floor. As Tyler brushed off his hands and started back to the little anteroom where the Ambassador stood guard over Lord Robert and the dead Kanehira, the old diplomat laid his hand on his subordinate's arm.

"See here, Tyler," he whispered hoarsely, "you can't stand by and let Murray kill himself this way. It's—it's ghastly."

Tyler smiled in a wintry way. After a pause he patted his astounded chief on the shoulder. "There! there! Good God! Mr Secretary!" he whispered soothingly. "Don't worry! Trust me to see this through."

Back in the room with the candles and corpse, Tyler appeared perfectly businesslike.

"Now then," he remarked briskly, "let's see. How many revolvers have we? Only two? Tut! tut! That's bad. Very bad. Most irregular. Frank, old man, would you mind trotting downstairs and getting another one? Perhaps the Ambassador will call down to the guard and direct him to give you his lethal weapon. Thank you, Mr Ambassador. That will do very nicely."

While Urquhart returned downstairs and the Ambassador uttered a stream of peremptory gutturals and sibilants over the banisters, Dennis went quickly over to Murray.

" See here," he whispered, " you've read *Stalky & Co.*, haven't you? What Englishman hasn't? Well, just remember that ' the bleating of the kid excites the tiger ' and keep your eye peeled for dear old Frank. All right? Well, ta! ta! No flowers by request and none of us can live for ever. Here's Frank with the extra gun. Let's see it."

Half hypnotized by Tyler's relentless volubility, Urquhart handed over the pistol.

" Just like mine," Dennis remarked. " A useful weapon. Hardly the thing for an elephant hunt but perfectly adequate for *felo de se*. Thirty-eight is a damned fine calibre. Not as messy as a forty-five nor yet so trivial as a twenty-two."

He snapped open the cylinder and spun it round.

" Quite right," he commented. " Every chamber charged, though one ought to be enough. Here you are, Robert," Tyler continued, stretching out his hands with a revolver in each. He spun them round on the trigger-guard, presenting the butts.

" Take your choice," he ordered. " If I may advise

you, I would suggest taking my revolver, the one in my right hand. It is, in fact, a sweet little weapon. Good! Now for orders. You, Robert, are going to sit down at that little table between the safe and the window and write your confession. Then the rest is up to you. Do you understand?"

"Quite," Murray assented briefly.

"Very well. Here, Frank, help me shift this late gentleman over by the window. There's just a shade too much local colour, as it were, in this setting. . . . Splendid! Now we will leave you. I will stand guard by the door into the hall, outside of course; and Frank will go into the next room and guard the connecting door behind those curtains. And if you should feel restless after making your confession, I may say that Frank and I are both prepared to shoot if you should try to escape. Good-bye, old man, and don't think too harshly of me. I'm sorry as the devil for this, but it's the only way out."

The Secretary went wordlessly up to the young Englishman, seized his hand and pressed it firmly, then turned away, his shoulders shaking.

"I say, Mr Secretary," Tyler suggested, "why don't you and the Ambassador go downstairs and wait? You might take Peggy down with you, too. This is no place for a girl."

The two old men set the candles on the top of the safe, where they balanced, guttering, casting long eerie shadows over the horrible little room. The shadows jumped and twitched and shifted, now squatting like toads in the corners, now darting out, now crouching back. The footsteps died away in the hall and down the stairs.

Urquhart held out his hand to Murray. " Old man," he said, " I can't tell you how I feel about this. It's a tough break all right and I—— Will you shake hands with me before you go ? "

Murray's eyes travelled contemptuously over the heavy features of the Press Adviser. A slow smile passed across his lips, and he stretched out his hand and grasped Urquhart's.

" Fortunes of war," he murmured. " See you later."

Dennis broke in on the embarrassing pause which followed.

" Now then," he said, " we can't keep them waiting downstairs. It's a quarter to twelve and I have only until midnight to get things cleared up. We'll allow you five minutes to do the job."

Tyler and Urquhart withdrew. The door closed. Murray was left alone. He stared at the revolver, which he had laid on the table, with the pen and paper

which Urquhart had brought. It seemed to have grown larger and larger, and the muzzle, which was pointed at him, was as deep and black as a well. He picked up the weapon and flicked open the cylinder. It was not loaded. . . . Hastily he laid the weapon down, went over to the window and lifted the dead valet in his arms. . . .

Outside in the hall Tyler closed the door firmly behind him. He turned to Urquhart.

" I'll take this door," he said. " You go round and take the connecting door. You won't mind going into the room where Hojo is, will you? "

Urquhart hesitated and then nodded.

" Right! " he assented. " It won't be long. Oh! by the way, what shall we do if he doesn't—er—act? "

Tyler thought.

" If he doesn't act within five minutes," he said, " it will always be possible for one of us to go in and —ah—assist him. But I think we'll be hearing a shot before then."

Urquhart nodded again. He became obsessed with an idea. It was a desperate idea and not a pleasant one. He tried to get it out of his head. He kept seeing a white-clad back bowed over a little writing-table in the flickering light of two tall tapers. He saw

a hand with a pistol reaching out from the curtains which covered a certain doorway. The hand held a revolver and the safe cast a black shadow so that you couldn't see the man's face. The man was walking noiselessly in stockinged feet. The pen kept scratching on the paper. The man crept nearer and nearer. He held the revolver close to the bowed head. A finger tightened on the trigger and the white back slumped forward over the table, sending a candle sprawling to the floor, rolling in a spluttering circle of hot wax and smoke. The man leaped noiselessly back into the shadow and behind the curtain. . . .

"Right!" he said again. "I'll wait five minutes and then, if nothing happens, I'll come round and consult you as to what to do. But I agree with you. He'll kill himself all right."

Urquhart tiptoed away, slipped into the next room and took up his station by the other door. Both he and Tyler reached for their revolvers, and waited.

Silence fell upon the Embassy and in the silence there was a faint throbbing, the beating of the wings of the angel of death. Death seemed over and under and round them. Death walked in the corridors and fumbled at the casements. Death stood in the doorways and whispered in the silences. A dead man lay

in the room where the young Chargé was passing his
allotted minutes. Two minutes had gone. Death lay
in the room where Urquhart crouched waiting, watching the widening sliver of light that crept in from the
door behind the curtains. At the end of the passage
a man lay unconscious, his head bloodied from a caress
of death's fingers, his breath rattling in his throat.
Downstairs, two old men, long on nodding terms with
death, sat waiting bleakly, while between them a
woman cried. In the basement, two men sat drinking
from a bottle, while a third lay in a stupor on the
floor. Inside and outside the building death had
woven a net. Death was everywhere. Four minutes
had gone . . .

Tyler was conscious of a sudden little tingle of his
skin, a shivering breath of anticipation. Four and a
half minutes had gone. Surely by now . . . Suddenly
the silence was broken by a single tragic crash, half
muffled, as a shot rang out in the little room, a shot
which was quickly deadened as the explosion broke
itself against yielding flesh and blood.

THE END OF THE PASSAGE

THE shot rang out like a confession of guilt. The long game of cross-purposes was at an end. Tyler sighed once deeply and tapped his finger nervously on the jamb of the door. He could hear a sudden exclamation from downstairs as Acorn's gruff voice inquired anxiously whether somebody hadn't fired a shot and what was the matter with the lights, anyhow.

Tyler gave a start. A hand was laid on his shoulder. It was Frank Urquhart. The Press Adviser's eyes gleamed in the dimness of the corridor.

" I know how you must feel," he purred. " Poor Murray! He did the decent thing at the end, after all. Don't you think we'd better go in and tidy up a bit before the others——"

Dennis nodded. " My dear old Frank," he said, " you're absolutely right. You go first. Do you mind? "

Urquhart opened the door boldly. The flicker of the tall candles was still peopling the room with creeping little shadows. As Dennis followed, he unobtrusively drew his revolver. Urquhart's, he noticed, was

in his hand. At the little table, half in shadow, a white-clad form was slumped down.

Urquhart glanced casually round. He noticed a curious lightish shadow by the window. He gave a swift, troubled glance at the dead man and then toward the body of the murdered valet. The body was gone. Puzzled, he drew nearer to the suicide. Suddenly he darted forward and twisted the head round. As he did so, a hoarse yell burst from his throat. He spun on his heel, waving his revolver in front of him, with a shaking hand and a wild glare in his eye.

"Where is he?" he shrieked shrilly. "Where *is* he?"

He turned savagely round. At that moment, Tyler's arm lunged out, as he thrust the barrel of his pistol hard against Urquhart's back.

" Put 'em up!" he ordered.

" Ditto!" drawled a voice, from the corner.

Urquhart's revolver clattered to the floor and his hands went over his head.

Murray slouched forward negligently, clad in his underwear.

" First time I've felt cool to-day," he remarked. " The bleating of the kid excites the tiger. I'll keep him covered while you tie him up."

Groaning inwardly at the exorbitant cost of tailored silk shirts, Tyler ripped off Urquhart's and neatly bound the Press Adviser's arms behind him.

" How'd you make out ? " Tyler inquired of Murray.

" Oh, it was easy enough, though a bit fast. I got my shirt on Kanehira but made a hash of the trousers. If you don't mind I'll retrieve 'em now. They're under the table. Keep him covered, will you ? "

" Yes," continued Murray, struggling into his now completely disreputable flannels, " I set him up in the chair, rolled over in the corner and waited. I didn't have to wait long. First thing I knew, Frank Urquhart had sneaked from behind those curtains round the safe, put his pistol under poor old Kanehira's ear, and let go. Then he disappeared and after a decent interval came in with you. And here we are ! "

" And here they are ! " Tyler added.

Framed in the doorway stood a terror-stricken group. The Ambassador alone was impassive. The Secretary was supporting Peggy Lawrence, and Acorn was craning his neck, with the uneasy expression of a man who expects to receive a snowball on the back of the head at any moment, but isn't quite sure when.

" By God! Murray!" was the Secretary's exclamation. "What's all this, hey?"

At his words, Peggy looked up and saw her lover alive. She rushed forward and flung herself into his arms.

As she did so, Urquhart suddenly wrenched his arms loose from the bonds, turned and hit Dennis cleanly on the point of the jaw, thrust through the group at the door and ran. Down the stairs he went, three steps at a time, and at the bottom, without losing his stride, he picked up the bronze Buddha and hurled it with terrific force at the Japanese guard. Not expecting the onset, the guard went down in a heap as fifty pounds of bronze struck him. Urquhart jerked the front door open and dashed out into the street. He was met, at the foot of the steps, by two hundred pounds of official brawn, concentrated in the fist of Captain Nichols.

" Hey, you!" grumbled the head of the Departmental Guards, " where yuh going?"

Urquhart described a complicated geometric curve, charitably called a parabola, and sprawled unconscious on the grass. Nichols unkindly took hold of his heels and dragged him up the steps into the Embassy.

" There!" he said. " Serves yuh damned well right

for tryin' to enter the United States without a passport. You're in Japan, young feller, and my orders is to keep you there."

"Captain, oh, my captain!" Tyler's anguished voice broke in on Nichols' oration. "Have you got such a thing as a pair of handcuffs? I'm afraid granny's knots aren't much good for tying up people."

"Sure I have," said Nichols. "Say, Mr Tyler, what's all the shootin'? Need any help?"

"Toss 'em here." Tyler commanded. "That was only target practice. The game's over. Call off your men and go home."

The handcuffs gleamed for a moment in the light of the arc, then fell with a jingle and unmusical clash in the inky pool of shadow inside the Embassy door. The door was swung shut and the handcuffs clicked into place on Urquhart's wrists, just as he began to recover consciousness. With the help of the perspiring and bewildered Acorn—the guard was still groaning by the overturned Buddha—Tyler half led, half carried the Press Adviser upstairs to the little room, where the Ambassador and the Secretary of State were awaiting explanations.

"You see, revered sirs," Tyler began easily, "here is your murderer. Mr Urquhart has very kindly

cleared up the crime for us, though not perhaps as he intended. His own actions have accused him so clearly that I do not think that there is any reasonable doubt of his guilt, unless we choose to revive for his benefit his own fond theory of an attack of homicidal mania."

"Stop beating round the bush, Tyler," the Secretary ordered. "Tell us what happened."

Tyler sighed, reproachfully. "Mr Urquhart got tired of waiting for Murray to commit suicide, so decided to assist him. In a word, to murder him. He walked in through that door into the next room—I had purposely stationed him on guard there—and fired a shot into the man who was sitting in the chair at the writing-desk. Fortunately, the man at the desk was not Lord Robert but was the late Kanehira, carefully placed in that position by Lord Robert, for reasons which will be obvious to us all. As you will notice, the light from these candles is rather dim and the table is partly in the shadow, so in the moment Mr Urquhart snatched to commit his crime he did not have the chance to verify whether it was Murray or his previous victim. Mr Urquhart then withdrew, convinced he had murdered the man in such a way that it would clearly be a case of suicide—a suicide which

would be the equivalent of a confession. Why was he so anxious to have Lord Robert out of the way? Because he knew that Lord Robert was innocent. How did he know Lord Robert was innocent? Because he knew he had planned the crime himself. . . . When Mr Urquhart discovered that his plan had miscarried, he lost complete control of himself, I regret to say, and implicated himself still further. The rest of his behaviour you saw for yourselves. Ask him if he has any explanation?"

The Ambassador eyed his American subordinate sternly. "Well, Mr Urquhart," he demanded, "have you anything to say?"

Urquhart said nothing, his eyes staring stonily across the room.

"You see," said Tyler, after a pause, "he has condemned himself."

"Yes, yes, yes!" blurted Acorn impatiently. "But that doesn't tell us why he did it."

Tyler smiled. "The whole thing was a ghastly mistake," he announced. "If it had gone off as scheduled, we would have had a little trouble solving it. As it is, simplicity itself."

"What was it?" the Secretary barked. "Tell it straight!"

"Yes, Mr Secretary," Tyler agreed patiently. "The fact is that both Mr Urquhart and Hiki are members of the Black Dragon Society, *n'est-ce pas*, Frank?"

Urquhart gave a slight shudder.

The Ambassador intervened. "But the Black Dragons would never——" he began excitedly.

"Of course they wouldn't," Tyler agreed. "That's just the trouble. We know their programme is to unite Asia against the West. They are shrewd enough to think clearly on a point like this. The plan was to kill, not Prince Hojo, but Lord Robert, under circumstances which would point to the Prince as the murderer. That would not only discredit the leader of the party for co-operation with the West, but would lead to the two Anglo-Saxon Powers taking the initiative in Asia. That in turn would have united Asia and put the blame on the West.

"Urquhart smuggled Hiki into the Embassy before the Prince's arrival, gave him a chance to see the valet whom the greatest actor of Japan was to impersonate, and together they killed him and put the body in the safe. They planned, in the confusion following the murder, for the false Kanehira to run out on the street for the police and to disappear. Subsequently, long

after he was missed, the real Kanehira would be found in the safe and the temporary presence of Hiki would never have been suspected.

" Here is what went wrong. Hiki had put knock-out drops in the drinks. You can get them at any drug-store. Prince Hojo and Murray were lying unconscious upstairs when the Secretary of State arrived. What Hiki did not know was that they had changed their position after he had left them with the drinks. Then Hiki went up to announce the Secretary of State. At the door of the room, he slipped a pair of those heavy cotton socks which are common for house wear in Japan over his shoes—he's wearing them now, so I know—so that you would not hear what followed.

" You heard him go upstairs, walk to the door of the coffee-room, pause respectfully—waiting presumably for a lull in the conversation which might be going on within—and then knock once. After a while you heard him knock again and then come down to report that the Prince did not answer.

" Actually, Hiki did not pause at the door, which he had left ajar. He walked directly across the room, seizing a poker from the fireplace as he did so. He had probably arranged the room so that it would be there. He then went up to the man whom he thought

was Lord Robert and hit him a terrific blow on the head. *That was the first knock!* You must remember that the room was dim, the shutters closed, and that Prince Hojo and Lord Robert were dressed almost exactly alike. They were not standing, so that the difference in height was not apparent, and remember, Hiki had to work fast. The whole business took him about ten seconds. He thought he had killed Lord Robert. Actually he had killed a member of the Imperial Family. He then returned to the door and closed it with the spring-lock on the inside. He probably covered the click of the lock by his second knock. Then he went downstairs to tell you that the door was closed and that there was no answer. While you were able to hear, as you thought, every move that he made, he was committing the crime right over your heads and you never suspected it. When he recovers consciousness, he will verify it for you. The poor chap was ready to kill for his country—we have all done that at one time or another—but he was over. whelmed with horror when he found that he had killed the Prince and that his escape was cut off.

" Then Frank Urquhart blew in, having built up a cast-iron alibi at the Country Club. When he found his retreat cut off, he decided to reverse the plot and

throw the blame on Lord Robert. That carried him into deep and dangerous waters. If a mere British Chargé was murdered, that called for diplomatic explanations and apologies and bred bad blood, which was part of the Black Dragon plan. But the murder of a Prince of the Imperial Family looked uncomfortably like war. You yourself know, Mr Ambassador, how even the ' Jiji Shimpo ' would react to such a crime and what use the Black Dragons would have made of it. Urquhart was desperate. He was in constant terror lest Hiki should give the show away, in remorse, and he was afraid of the vengeance the Black Dragons would take on him for having bungled. He *had* to prove Lord Robert guilty and he *had* to escape, or he was done for. It was *that* I was building on, principally on suspicion, and I relied upon one or the other of them to make a false move. They did."

The Ambassador sighed. " Yes, Mr Urquhart ? " he asked again.

Urquhart rolled his head helplessly from side to side. " I have nothing to say."

" Then," the Ambassador concluded, " you had better go downstairs."

" Wait a moment, Mr Ambassador," Tyler interposed. " What are you planning to do ? "

Viscount Kondo shrugged his shoulders. " Finish,"
he remarked succinctly.

" May I suggest a better way? " the Chief of the
C.P.I. asked anxiously.

" Yes, Mr Tyler? " was the toneless query.

" Let him go! Let Hiki go! You know they are
guilty, although you may never get either of them to
admit it. If you execute them now, it is mercy to
them. The Black Dragons, from what I've heard,
have a way of treating those of their members who
fail. Let them go! They will never know at what
hour of the day or night they will meet their end.
They will only know that it will come and will come
soon. Let them go and they will be dead men within
a month."

The Ambassador nodded and his lips twisted into a
bleak, mirthless smile. " You are right, Mr Tyler.
They shall go. First I shall send Hiki to the hospital
for treatment. It would be sad if he should die just
now. Then I will let him go. Mr Urquhart shall go
now."

MORNING AFTER

THE discreet private ambulance whirred away through the silent streets bearing Hiki to the hospital. Urquhart's reluctant footsteps had died away, echoing strangely loud beneath the dusty elms and humming arc-lights. The guards had dispersed to their several private employments, leaving only two standing watch over the two fatal rooms on the second story of the Embassy, where lay the bodies of two men who had died for their country.

" I must send a full report of this to Tokio," muttered the Ambassador. His sallow face was scarred with weariness and his eyes were dull with fatigue. " If only we had not sent the first telegram."

" That's all right, Mr Ambassador," Tyler explained blithely. " Your first telegram hasn't gone yet. When I gave the order to set a guard round the Embassy, it naturally included orders to the cable company to hold up your telegram. And don't let them collect tolls for triple priority, either. You have to watch out for little tricks like that."

The Ambassador nodded. " Very clever," he commented. " You were very sure of yourself."

Tyler smirked. " The Secretary of State will bear me out——" he began.

" There's many a true word spoken in jest, Tyler," his superior agreed. " And you'll be unconscious when I bear you out, if you don't quit your damned self-satisfied superiority. You're a fool for luck and that's all."

" Luck," Tyler murmured, in an inaudible protest, " is just another word for genius. I forget who said that. Does it matter? "

" Very good," agreed the Ambassador. " I will send my report to Tokio and then I must resign my post. It is the only way I can atone."

The Secretary started. " Surely, Viscount," he protested, " you are not going to——" His voice trailed off into silence.

The Ambassador nodded his head gravely.

" May I make a suggestion? " Tyler began eagerly.

The Secretary and Acorn turned on their subordinate, with a ' What, again? ' attitude in their bearing.

Tyler did not wait for a reply, but rattled on. " May I suggest that you send a cablegram to Tokio

now, giving a full account of what happened, suggesting an official version to be given to your Press, and requesting instructions as to the action which your traditions suggest to you. You see, sir, you are more useful to your country and may serve it better by staying at this post where we know you and like you than by resigning now. I know it is hard for you to consider this, but I believe, sir, that your Government will feel as I do."

The Secretary turned eagerly to the Ambassador. " He's right, your Excellency. Your Government's interest should determine your action now."

The Ambassador reflected for a long time. " I shall ask them," he announced at last, " and I shall await their answer."

The telegram was hastily drafted and encoded and sent to Tokio, triple priority. There was nothing to do but wait. Tyler, quite unabashed, went upstairs and had a nap on the sofa in the upper hall. Acorn drifted down to the basement once more and joined Joe O'Connor in a friendly game, in the course of which he lost a great deal of money and didn't care. The Secretary and the Ambassador drowsed wearily in their chairs. Out in the garden, Lord Robert had long since given up the attempt of persuading Peggy that

he had not captured the culprit with his bare hands
and had compromised by telling her about his family
and how much she would like his mother. . . .

Toward dawn came the answer from Tokio, signed
by the Emperor himself. Viscount Kondo was not to
resign. The Ambassador was to sign the agreement
with the British Chargé in Prince Hojo's stead. The
official version was to be that Prince Hojo had died of
heat prostration and that Kanehira had killed himself
for grief for his master. Every precaution must be
taken to prevent the truth from becoming known. In
the meantime, the Japanese police would deport every
known member of the Black Dragons, which by Order
in Council was to be instantly proscribed as an outlaw
organization. As soon as the agreement was signed,
the Ambassador was authorized to give it to the
American Press. The text would be released in Tokio
at the same time. And so on and so on, in the im-
memorial manner of bureaucracies the world over.

It was a dishevelled and disreputable group which
assembled in the large reception room to witness the
signing of an historic document, the agreement which
brought Japan into the Anglo-American naval alliance
as a full partner in that great diplomatic undertaking
to maintain the peace of the world. There was Bill

Strong, still red-eyed and unsteady from his potations, but with the shrewdest brain in journalism taking in the scene; Peggy Lawrence, looking radiant and utterly ignorant of what was happening; Dennis Tyler, red-haired, unshaven, in the wreck of what had once been an immaculate morning suit; James B. Acorn, Assistant Secretary of State, looking like a Corn Belt politician out on a party with the boys; the Secretary of State, five foot six of diplomatic dynamite disguised as a peppery little old man who walked as though the ground were red-hot and who spoke as though he lived on ginger; Viscount Kondo, suave, silent, unsmiling, as individual and as Asiatic as a curved ceremonial sword; Lord Robert Murray, somehow cool and immaculate underneath garments that looked as though he were attending a fancy-dress ball in the garb of a tramp.

The pens squeaked slightly on the parchment paper of the treaty. Copies were exchanged and initialled, hands were shaken, and the deed was done. The billion and a half of mites which proudly peopled a spinning particle in the chill spaces between the stars would live out their momentary lives in peace for one, two, and perhaps three generations, because of that morning's work.

EPILOGUE

A COOL wind came sweeping down from the north. It drew coolness and strength from the mountains of the Blue Ridge, swept down over Frederick, and leaped from hill-top to hill-top of the rolling country, ruffling the little runs which furrowed a peaceful land, passing in green lovely waves over the fields of corn. The wind came down from the north and calmed the fever of the city. The heat wave had broken and autumn beckoned across the lap of summer. The wind blew on, down deep into the south, across the Potomac, past Fredericksburg and Chancellorsville, to Richmond, Appomattox, and still on, cooling the weary land to the Blue Gulf and finding a country that was everywhere at peace because it had built its peace on power, power that was crushing, power that was final, power that fertilized a nation of men of many minds to live and to work as one.

" Just the same, I wish somebody had noticed the fact that I solved the whole nasty mess for them before midnight, as I said I would," complained the Chief of the C.P.I. " And I hope that Acorn

remembers that I won a ten-dollar bet from him," he added.

He sighed, looked at Murray and grinned morosely. " I suppose," he remarked bitterly, " that you expect me to buy a new frock-coat for your wedding. Well, I won't do it. You can be married in flannels, or not at all."